THE SMILING STRANGER

In the 1870s, pretty Amy Felstead was 'companion' to her domineering cousin, Elspeth, who tried to steer her into marriage with man-about-town Charles Henthorne. So, when Amy learned that she had inherited a gold mine in Australia, she snatched at the chance of escape. Alas, reality was far removed from the dream. Soon, Amy was to find herself in deadly danger before a secret enemy was unmasked and she was able to plan for the future with a man who truly loved her.

Books by Nara Lake
Published by The House of Ulverscroft:

THE SECRET MAN
LOST WOMAN

NARA LAKE

THE SMILING STRANGER

Complete and Unabridged

ULVERSCROFT
Leicester

First published in Great Britain

First Large Print Edition
published 2000

All characters and incidents in this
story are fictitious, and the town of
Firebrace and its inhabitants have never
existed except in the author's imagination.

British Library CIP Data

Lake, Nara
The smiling stranger.—Large print ed.—
Ulverscroft large print series: romance
1. Love stories
2. Large type books
I. Title
823.9'14 [F]

ISBN 0–7089–4217–2

Published by
F. A. Thorpe (Publishing)
Anstey, Leicestershire
Set by Words & Graphics Ltd.
Anstey, Leicestershire
Printed and bound in Great Britain by
T. J. International Ltd., Padstow, Cornwall

This book is printed on acid-free paper

1

She was leaving Firebrace. Soon, all that had happened there would be a memory as she was carried away eastwards, clinging to the leather strap provided to ease the jolts as the coach lurched over the travesty of a road. Early that morning, a thunderstorm accompanied by heavy rain had swept across the area, so that new potholes and occasional quagmires would add to the discomforts of the journey between Firebrace and the railhead.

There was all the usual last-minute activity outside the coaching office. Luggage was being stacked on the roof, and, in between, the poor and hardy passengers would take their chance against the elements, in this case, steamy sunshine. There were always a few idlers with nothing better to do than stand about and watch the preparations until, at last, the driver climbed up to his seat, took the reins, released the brake, and sent his powerful horses forward under the expert cracking of his long whip.

Amy leaned back against the leather, feeling the hotness through her muslin dress, and closing her eyes for a moment. She had come across the world to Firebrace, and nothing in her life could ever be the same again. Firebrace the town, and Firebrace the man, would be with her forever, haunting her dreams and pulling at her heart.

It had all started, as do many changes, with a visit from a stranger. How well she remembered the occasion, on that water-colour English spring day, soft and pastel, the way this other land could never be. She had been cutting early blooms, and had just pricked her finger on a rose thorn. As she stood there sucking at the puncture, Emily, the parlourmaid, slightly disapproving as she always was of the young woman who was neither servant nor guest, had come from the house and told her that a Mr Sturrock wished to see her.

Amy had no notion whom Mr Sturrock might be, and glanced down at his card with considerable curiosity. He was, it transpired, one of the Messrs Sturrock of the law firm of Sturrock, Rench and Sturrock. He had also come from London, a distance of twenty miles, to pay this call.

She could only suppose that the visit had something to do with her allowance, which had not been forthcoming for a number of weeks. It had come to her automatically after her mother had died three years previously, the matter being handled by a firm of solicitors in Melbourne, Australia, for the deep bitterness between her parents had caused a rift beyond healing. The terms of the separation had stated that she, Amy, must go with her mother, and her father had never corresponded with her directly after that.

Mr Sturrock was about forty, thin to the point of being cadaverous, and in his black frock coat, more like an undertaker than a solicitor. He shook her hand with a member as dry as his appearance, and she invited him to be seated, although if she had been watching him more closely, she would have observed in those sunken eyes a passing gleam of appreciation.

Amy Felstead was at this time just past twenty-one years of age. She was a little taller than average, but not too much, so that there was about her a willowy grace, emphasised by the blue striped dress with its frilled apron front drawn to the back to form a gentle bustle. Her features were too soft and small to be fashionable in this age when handsome, rather than pretty, women were admired, but her complexion was good, her brows well marked over fine blue eyes, and her brown hair, with its rich hint of

3

chestnut, was abundant and dressed without padding.

'I'm afraid,' said Mr Sturrock, after clearing his throat, 'that I bring bad news.' This was uttered in a professionally lugubrious tone, and he paused, as if awaiting her reaction.

She looked at him, steadily.

'It's my father, isn't it?' she asked, clearly and calmly. 'He has died.'

Mr Sturrock seemed relieved that he was not to be treated to swoonings and hysterics, and nodded.

'Yes. I'm very sorry, Miss Felstead. The information reached our firm only yesterday from the solicitors handling your father's estate in Melbourne. I'm surprised that no one had informed you more directly.'

'How did he die?' Then she felt obliged to add an explanation, in case he thought her cold-blooded. 'I'd not seen my father since I was eight years old. He and my mother were legally separated. We never corresponded.'

'I see.' Mr Sturrock thawed out slightly. 'It is my understanding that he was killed in a mine accident, Miss Felstead. About three months ago. There is no point in wasting time. He left his entire estate to you. There is, I gather, some property in Melbourne itself, and a gold-mine and other property in the vicinity of a town called — um — Firebrace, which I believe to be some miles out of Melbourne in the Australian colony of Victoria.'

Trust him to be killed in a mine, thought his daughter, not very sentimentally. Gold-mines had been his entire life, to the exclusion of ordinary family existence and the welfare of his dependants, as her mother had told her so often. Amy had been born within a stone's throw of one of father's mines, in California, and had then been taken as a babe in arms across the Pacific to Australia. Practically all she could remember of the latter place was tents and gold-mines, and her mother complaining incessantly of the dreadful discomforts.

It was small wonder that Mrs Felstead decided that she had had enough, and had returned to England with her small daughter. There had been times when they had been quite comfortably fixed, and could have used the profits from the latest venture to settle into a more regular mode of life, but Amy's father could not resist the lure of gold. A hint of a new strike somewhere, and he had to be off, plunging their savings into leases and equipment, gambling as surely as if he had sat down to a game of poker with all his worldly goods as the stake.

5

'The Royal Edward Mine,' the legal man said, and Amy, despite the solemnity of the occasion, almost laughed.

How like her father! He had spent most of his adult life away from his native country, yet always the names of his mines were absolutely patriotic. She remembered, vaguely, the Balaclava which had commemorated the famous Crimean battle. That had been near Bendigo, in Victoria, and the Queen Victoria, Edmund's interest at the time of her birth, had been in California, advertising to all and sundry that the promoter was a true-blue Briton.

'I understand, from our Melbourne informants, that the Royal Edward shows considerable promise. Assays made on samples taken from the mine show a very high yield of gold.'

Amy wanted to pinch herself, and at the same time, tears prickled behind her eyelids at the sheer, cruel irony of it. After a lifetime of seeking that elusive Eldorado, poor father had perished in the mine which promised to fulfil his dreams. Now she, Amy, who could barely remember that dashing and ebullient man whose outward show of opulence had so often belied straitened circumstances, was an heiress!

Life in England, for herself and her mother,

6

had been far from affluent. There was the allowance, which to do father justice, had arrived regularly, but it did little more than cover the barest necessities. There had to be a boarder, and numerous miserable economies to help keep up some sort of appearance before mother's family. Fortunately, for mother's pride, most of them lived in distant corners of England and were rarely seen, but Uncle Theo and Cousin Elspeth were uncomfortably close at hand. Uncle Theo, who was now an invalid confined to a bathchair, had always disapproved of Edmund Felstead.

'A loose fish' was his kindlier description. On other occasions he referred to his niece's husband as an 'unmitigated blackguard' or a 'conniving rogue', whereupon Amy's mother, resenting this insult to her judgement, would stalk out of the house, swearing never to enter it again. Elspeth Fordyce, a year older than her cousin Catherine, and unwed, was the peacemaker. A plain, solidly built woman who had long since accepted her single fate, she was much given to good works, and when Mrs Felstead had died of a chest infection, she had instantly suggested that Amy should make her home with herself and Uncle Theo.

'Do stay with us, for a little while, until

you make up your mind what to do,' insisted Cousin Elspeth. 'You're very young, and I know that your poor mother would be greatly comforted to know that we are caring for you.'

'I should like to go to my father,' timidly suggested Amy, still dazed by grief.

'But where is your father?'

This was a very good question, and as Cousin Elspeth further pointed out, to locate Edmund Felstead, a wanderer who seldom stayed anywhere longer than six months, could take at least a year.

'So you must stay with us,' insisted Elspeth. 'You're too young, Amy, to be venturing across the world on your own. And I *need* you. I'm not offering you charity, my dear. You know that I can never keep up with my correspondence, nor find anything when I want it, and . . . Oh, Amy, dearest, do come for a little while.'

Thus, Amy became a sort of secretary to Elspeth with all her foreign missions and improvement schemes for the deserving poor, and, between times, a sounding board for Uncle Theo. She was also, she was extremely aware, the intended wife of one Charles Henthorne.

'Do you think,' said Amy, very slowly, and rather softly, as Mr Sturrock sat immobile in a chair opposite hers, 'that I should go to Australia myself?'

It was the luckiest of chances that Cousin Elspeth was out at a meeting, and that Uncle Theo was having his afternoon nap. Amy knew that if Elspeth had heard her speaking of the possibility of leaving the country, she would immediately look dreadfully hurt, blinking her eyes rapidly until she recovered herself and forced a brave expression. The worst of living with relatives, Amy had learnt, was that one came to know all their foibles so well.

'Dear Amy,' Elspeth would say, trying to hide the tremor in her voice, 'do you think it wise? You know that your poor mother — and it is to be hoped that she and your father have become reunited on a higher, more spiritual plane — insisted on bringing you home from those outlandish places because of the strain on your health.'

It would have been hard to tell Cousin Elspeth that she, Amy, had been almost fiendishly healthy in those outlandish places, and that the story had been a fabrication by her mother to help cover up the truth of a disastrous marriage.

I must make a decision *now*, thought Amy quickly, as the lawyer glanced at her in a querying but kindly fashion.

'You are of age, Miss Felstead?'

'Yes.'

'I must point out that there are business matters — you may find them difficult.'

'And why should that be, Mr Sturrock?'

Amy could see that she had startled Mr Sturrock, and this gave her a certain inward pleasure. For a long time, she had wondered why she was generally treated as if she were slightly simple-minded, but lately it had occurred to her that the reason was that she was a woman, and a pretty young woman. She was expected to be soft and yielding and forever giving way to the superior wisdom of the male.

'Miss Felstead, it is most unusual to — um — well, young ladies like yourself have no knowledge of business complexities.'

'But my signature could be required on papers eventually?'

Poor Mr Sturrock was becoming more nonplussed by the moment. He took it for granted that one could not judge a masculine book by its cover, that a lofty forehead and keenly penetrating gaze could conceal a minute intelligence, and a low brow and a dreamy mien a sharp and questing mind. There was, however, he had long assumed, a rule of thumb for ladies. The prettier, the sillier. Only the plain members of the sex sought refuge in brains.

He nodded.

'Then I shall travel to Melbourne to see to everything myself. I have a feeling, Mr Sturrock, that is what my father would have desired.' Even as she uttered the words, Amy felt the first flutterings of trepidation. She could imagine the general reaction to this decision, but it had been made, and she continued speaking calmly, requesting that Mr Sturrock should arrange her passage at the earliest possible date.

She knew that otherwise, she would be talked out of this rash venture, and that, before she knew what had happened, she would be married to Charlie Henthorne.

2

Cousin Elspeth Fordyce's thwarted maternal
instincts had been saved to be expended,
when hope of producing a family of
her own had passed, on her younger
relatives. This could be said to be divided,
unequally, between Amy Felstead and Charlie
Henthorne at a ratio of about forty-sixty. Like
Amy, Charlie was the child of a cousin, a
colonel in the Indian Army who had lived
out of England for many years. Charlie
had shown liking for neither the Army nor
India, and having an income from his mother
which amounted, Elspeth said, to about two
thousand pounds a year, was able to lead
the sort of idle and frivolous life for which
his intellect and abilities suited him.

Elspeth was fond of Amy in a slightly
domineering, I-know-what's-best way, but
she doted upon Charlie, who at this time
was thirty years of age. He was handsome,
quite tall, and slenderly prepossessing, and
being given to all the latest fads in hirsute
adornment, Amy had the suspicion always
that she did not really know what he looked
like. She did not dislike him, and could

12

even admit to an affection for him, but it was the tolerant, shallow feeling one might have for an agreeable, but not particularly well-behaved, pet animal.

Ever since Amy had taken up her abode there, Charlie had been a regular caller at the house, for, balanced against a taste for (so Amy had overheard the bootboy telling the groom) *tableaux vivants* and well-built young women in pink tights, Mr Henthorne possessed sufficient kindliness to visit a grumpy old man who was now almost a prisoner within his household. Uncle Theo enjoyed Charlie's company, Amy gathered from the bellows of laughter emerging from behind closed doors, and she suspected that Charlie brought with him from London the latest scraps of scandal and the newest saucy anecdotes of the kind quite unfit for a lady's ears.

Lately, there had been a change, Uncle Theo took second place, and Amy was left in no doubt that Charlie travelled all the way from his rooms in a fashionable part of Town to see her. Elspeth was delighted.

'Couldn't be better!' she declared. 'You know one another well, and you're not related by blood.' (Amy and Charlie were both of them from different branches of Elspeth's family tree.) 'And you would be well placed, Amy, dearest. Oh, my dear, how I've prayed that this might happen.'

She did not say that Amy was just the type of steady young woman Charlie needed to make him settle down. Amy hoped that Charlie's interest was a passing phase, but the night prior to Mr Sturrock's visit, after two weeks of unmistakable intentions, the worst had happened.

Despite her attempts at discouragement, Charlie had proposed. Like all the best proposals, it had taken place in the conservatory, whither Amy had fled when she had heard her suitor announced, in the vain hope that he would be button-holed by Uncle Theo. Uncle Theo was very annoyed by something which Mr Gladstone had said, and longing for a male sounding board.

Charlie, however, was in no mood to be diverted by Uncle Theo's political opinions, and had found her almost straight away. It was not a very large conservatory, and as she moved to escape his fervent addresses, the alarmed girl had knocked over a potted fern, which had providentially landed heavily on Charlie's left shoe. A bruised big toe had a very calming effect, and she insisted that he sit and chat with Uncle Theo whilst she resettled the fern in its pot. Uncle Theo began one of his long discourses on

the folly of abolishing the sale of officers'
commissions. The Army, he declared, would
be led henceforth by lower-class bounders
with no idea of controlling the ranks, and
the nation would live to rue the day.

Although Charlie favoured Amy with
piteous and languishing glances, he could
not escape Uncle Theo, and the time soon
arrived when he had to leave in order to
catch his train up to Town.

As he left, he had pressed Amy's hand,
stared deep into her not very responsive blue
eyes from over his flowing fair moustache,
and uttered a sickly sigh.

'Until Sunday, dearest Amy,' he had
breathed, whilst she tried hard to suppress
a giggle. 'I shall hear your answer then.'

'Well?' demanded Elspeth as soon as
Charlie had been driven away to the station.

'I'm sorry about the fern,' said Amy, with
a brave attempt at guilelessness. 'Your lovely
Italian pot is cracked, I'm afraid,'

'Oh, don't worry about the wretched plant.
Did Charlie . . . ?'

Cousin Elspeth was right at her side,
breathing quite as heavily as Charlie had, her
pudgy hand with its collection of trumpery
rings clutching Amy's arm. Denied romance
herself, she had to live vicariously on the
emotions of others.

'Yes, he proposed.' Amy tried to sound cool, but the other woman's intensity worried her. 'Nothing is settled.'

Elspeth's hand dropped away.

'Oh,' she said, very disappointed. 'Amy, dearest, he does love you. For so long, he had hidden it. He told me himself, only a week ago. He felt that he was not worthy of you. He felt that some might think that as he is rather . . .'

A fool, thought Amy, ruthlessly, but kept this to herself.

'Aimless,' continued Elspeth, 'that he dare not aspire to your hand. I told him, from my heart, dearest Amy, that *you* would provide the purpose, and that your example must inspire him to reach for the heights of which he is truly capable.'

Formerly, Cousin Elspeth had never actually put into words her real ambitions for Amy, but now her young relative saw her destiny all too clearly. Amy had to keep Charlie on the straight and narrow path, Amy had to make a man out of him, Amy had to turn Charlie into a solid citizen who did not patronise *tableaux vivants*, bet on racehorses, and generally lead a shiftless life.

Amy kept silent, not wishing to be overwhelmed by the gush of sentimental arguments which Elspeth could produce when she desired her own way, but she lay awake a long time that night, sorting out her situation, and trying to decide upon the best course to take. Nicely brought-up young women were in such a difficult position if they had little money of their own.

She thought of the letters, always unanswered, which she had written to her father, care of his Melbourne solicitors, and wept a little into her pillow. However final the break between himself and her mother, why did he keep this silence towards his daughter?

Now, less than twenty-four hours later, a miracle had happened, and the road to escape stretched wide and straight before her. She was of age. She had a fortune awaiting her in Australia.

Uncle Theo's reaction was to expound upon bushrangers and convicts and someone called Esmond who had been sent to the colonies three decades earlier because he was a black sheep — a scug, Uncle Theo called him — and paid to keep away. Cousin Elspeth, as Amy had expected, immediately looked hurt and brave.

'But, dearest Amy, you don't know this man, this Mr Sturrock. Don't you think it very odd that no one else has taken it upon himself to tell you the sad news of your father's death? One would have expected that a friend — and even your poor father must have had friends — would have undertaken this task, however trying and sorrowful.'

Amy wondered, not for the first time, whether Elspeth secretly rehearsed these speeches, of which she had suitable samples for all occasions.

'I'm sure that Mr Sturrock is just what he appears to be. After all, why should anyone pretend to be a member of a perfectly respectable firm of solicitors and go to the bother of travelling from London to tell me that my father is dead?'

Even Cousin Elspeth could not answer this.

'My father has left me property in Victoria. I believe it includes a house, completely furnished.'

'But you cannot live there alone!'

'I'm sure that I shall find a suitable housekeeper. Or I may let the house and take lodgings. It shall depend on how I find things.'

'And where is this house?'

'In a little town called Firebrace, west of Melbourne.'

'Firebrace! What an impossible name.'

'There are a lot of impossible names in Australia, Elspeth. Now, don't fret. Most likely, I shall see to it that things are settled, and return almost immediately to England.'

Elspeth began to cry.

The only way to cope was to be firm, however much she was tempted to weaken, to remind herself that although Uncle Theo and Cousin Elspeth had given her a home, they had also found her very useful. She read aloud to Uncle Theo when he was too bored to do it himself. She managed all Elspeth's more tiresome correspondence and poured tea for missionaries, and arranged flowers and supervised the servants and undertook errands, allowing Elspeth all the more time for loftier pursuits. As she had told Mr Sturrock, she was of age, and besides, within Amy's soft and pretty body there was a great deal of her father, that restless and adventurous man who had spent a lifetime seeking what lay beyond the next corner, and who had died, twelve thousand miles away, in an obscure hamlet called Firebrace.

★ ★ ★

'Dash it all,' said Charlie, 'you can't be serious. Dash it all.'

He was so overwrought that he dropped the monocle he had been sporting over the past week. As far as anyone knew, there was

19

nothing wrong with his eyesight, but Charlie was always in the forefront when it came to adopting new affectations.

It was Friday afternoon, and the two young people were sitting in the arbour, whither Charlie had steered Amy when he had arrived after receiving that urgent telegram from Elspeth. Amy usually did her best to avoid being alone with Charlie, but on this occasion a few moments' thought convinced her that it would be easier to cope with Elspeth and Mr Henthorne separately.

'Charlie, do try to understand. My father and I were strangers for many years, but I am sure that he wished me to take over my inheritance myself.'

The words sounded trite, but how could she explain her desire to reach out towards her father by entering his house and taking over his affairs herself? Equally difficult to express was her yearning to escape, not only from Charlie, but from the confined and ordered life within the Fordyce household.

'Your father,' spluttered Charlie, jamming his monocle back into place, 'never cared a fig about you while he was alive. Let those lawyer fellows puzzle their heads over what's to be done. That's why they're paid, dash it all! Dreadful country, Australia. Vulgar people. Met a fellow from Melbourne a couple of weeks ago when I was coming down from Town. Shouldn't have been allowed in a first-class carriage! You can't go there! Impossible! Place was settled by criminals.'

'Oh, fiddlesticks! We have criminals here, too. What about the burglary over at the Grange last month? And that dreadful man who beat his wife to death last year? And that poor man who was found by the railway line? Colonel Harris told Uncle Theo that no one knows who he is, and that he could have been knocked on the head. I think I shall be much safer in the wilds of Australia!'

'Bushrangers,' said Charlie, darkly. 'Infested with 'em.'

Then he seemed to remember something, and took her hand, holding it so tightly and coming so close that she was afraid that he meant to kiss her.

'And what about us, eh? Practically engaged, dash it all. You can't go off and leave me in the lurch. Feelings and all that.'

'Charlie, you'll soon find someone else. Someone who cares more deeply about you than I ever could. I'm sorry, Charlie, but I wouldn't have accepted you even if this hadn't happened!'

'Oh, dash it.' He released her hand and

looked so crestfallen that for an instant Amy felt herself weakening. 'Well,' he continued, trying hard to be cheerful, 'mustn't be a bounder. Can't force my attentions.'

'I am fond of you, Charlie, and I always think of you as one of my friends. But I'm sorry. That is as far as it goes.'

'Don't get yourself tied up in Australia. I'll still hope, y'know.'

'I won't tie myself up in Australia, Charlie. I'm in no hurry to marry.'

Charlie kissed her and, after the first surprise, she found herself thinking that Charlie must have had a lot of practice. He was very good at it, and the experience was quite agreeable.

'Only chance I'll ever have if you decide to stay in the colonies,' he commented, sorrowfully, as he stood up. 'Better rush off to catch my train. Dinner engagement tonight.'

It was an enormous relief to know that Charlie Henthorne was resigned, partly, to accepting the situation. Elspeth went on being hurt, but with so many preparations for her voyage to be made, Amy had little time to brood over this.

Mr Sturrock, who had reminded her so much of an undertaker the first time they met, proved to be competent and helpful. He arranged her passage on a full-rigged clipper, the *Parthenope*, known for record-breaking voyages almost as spectacularly swift as those of the famed *Thermopylae*.

With memories, which adulthood had not blurred, of a fearsome trip from Australia to Britain via Cape Horn, Amy would have preferred to travel by steamer through the Suez Canal, but no lady's berth was available for two months. However, as Mr Sturrock pointed out, the new crack sailing ships provided a fair degree of comfort for passengers, the outward-bound Cape of Good Hope route was by no means as dangerous as the homecoming Cape Horn 'easting' run, and the extra days necessarily spent at sea were offset by missing the extremely hot conditions of the Red Sea section of the Suez voyage.

She was a little disappointed at missing the chance of a side trip to the wonders of Ancient Egypt, but on the other hand, as Mr Sturrock said, there would be no delays at tedious coaling stations, where often there was little to interest the traveller. So, she fell in with his arrangement, but privately she determined that when she returned it would be by steamer through the Canal. Child though she had been at the time, her recollections of every loose object crashing about the ship, the wind screaming through the rigging, and days spent battened down below hatches in those high latitudes were sufficient to make Amy resolve never, never to travel via Cape Horn again.

Elspeth insisted on accompanying Amy and Mr Sturrock to the docks. Earlier, Amy had farewelled Uncle Theo.

'Hum,' he had said. 'Think you're making a mistake, me girl, but hope I'm proved wrong. Not that I blame you. No fun for a youngster living with a couple of old fogies like Elspeth and myself. You're a good girl, Amy. More sense than your mother, and your father too, as far as that goes. What a handsome fellow he was! Years older than your poor mother, God rest her soul.'

'I'll write to you, Uncle Theo, and tell you everything.'

'Don't expect to see you again,' announced Uncle Theo, gloomily. 'I'm seventy-two, you know, two years past my allotted span.'

Then the old man grinned, slyly.

'Don't blame you for knocking back Charlie, me girl. Not that I've anything against the lad. A bit of a featherweight, that's all. Elspeth dotes on him, that's the trouble. She should've married and had young 'uns of her own. Charlie ain't right for you, Amy, but it's no use arguing with Elspeth. She always did want her own way.'

Amy bent over and kissed his bald head, feeling more warmth for Uncle Theo than ever before. Too often, he was just a grumpy, demanding old man, embittered at being confined to a chair as the consequence of a fall from a horse whilst pursuing his lifelong passion of hunting.

It was a relief that Charlie did not come to see her off. Charlie, providentially, had a bad cold and was staying in his bed under the care of his manservant.

'He does love you,' said Elspeth, dabbing her eyes with a handkerchief. 'Oh, Amy, dearest, how can you be so cruel?'

Amy, in the emotion of the moment, did feel cruel and mean and quite ashamed, but suddenly her eyes caught Mr Sturrock's, and unbelievably, one of the solicitor's lids lowered slightly.

3

Sixty-one days after passing Land's End, she arrived at Port Melbourne, and was agreeably surprised to be met on Sandridge Pier by a Mr Parker, a member of the firm handling her father's estate. He had already received intelligence, per a mail steamer which had arrived a fortnight before, that she was on her way, and he had booked her a room at Scott's Hotel, which, he assured her, was a thoroughly respectable establishment.

He was a jovial, stout, matter-of-fact, middle-aged man, and Amy quickly felt at her ease with him. The following morning, she kept her appointment at his chambers, and he began explaining the details of the late Edmund Felstead's estate.

'Your father did not discuss his personal affairs with me, Miss Felstead. Our firm had only lately begun to handle his legal business. Actually, I believe that your father spent some time in Queensland, moving about a great deal, which no doubt is why you could not reach him by letter. However, he preferred the climate here in the south. His Firebrace venture was undertaken only a few months before his death. Now, Miss Felstead, I'm afraid that what I am about to tell you may be unpalatable.'

Amy felt a sinking sensation behind the sash of her dress. Later, she would analyse her response to Mr Parker's statement, and realise, for the first time, just how her mother felt when yet another of her father's end-of-the-rainbow finds turned out to be dross.

'Your father's estate, Miss Felstead, is quite impressive, on paper, at any rate. He owned some property here in Melbourne, cottages which are let out for rental. There is also a sizable amount of money invested in sterling bonds. This, at least, is in the clear, and provided the allowance which went first to your mother and, later, to yourself.'

'What about the mine?' asked Amy, still unable to understand the reason for Mr Parker's solemn warning.

'Ah, yes. The Royal Edward. This is located near the township of Firebrace, which lies some distance west of Ballarat, Miss Felstead. There is a house in the township which is included in the estate, and, fortunately, your father purchased this himself about three months before his death.'

'Is the mine in production?'

From Amy's childhood, phrases drifted back, the daily talk of the goldfields. A shaft. A new lead. A red flag on a miner's claim which meant that gold was being found. Mullock, the clay, gravel and rock from a mine, brought up to the surface, and dumped into mounds which arose, sterile and grassless, about every goldfield's site. Panning was washing dirt through by hand in a tin dish, so that any gold would be left in the bottom.

'Not at present. Your father was merely exploring the possibilities when he met his death. Very sad. There had been a very heavy downpour, and some of the supports were weakened by seepage and there was a fall . . . ' His voice trailed off for a few moments, respectfully, before resuming its briskness. 'The Royal Edward had been worked earlier, but the original company could not afford the machinery needed for crushing operations, and sold out quite cheaply, I believe, to the Firebrace family, on whose land the mine is situated.'

'Firebrace? Do you mean that there are actually *people* of that name?'

Mr Parker now looked decidedly uncomfortable, as if seeking the kindest way to broach an unpleasant subject. He cleared his throat and, taking a deep breath, proceeded.

'Yes, I'm afraid so, Miss Felstead. The site of the township was the Firebrace homestead block thirty years ago, built when old Mr Firebrace took up his run back in the very early days. The family moved soon after gold was discovered, practically in their own front garden, and built their present homestead which, I believe, is a regular mansion. Miss Felstead, I'm afraid that the Firebrace family and your father were at loggerheads.'

'You mean because the Royal Edward is on their land? I don't understand how this can be, Mr Parker.'

Amy was quite mystified, but underneath she had the knowledge that this was the catch, that the wonderful piece of good fortune which had come her way was too good to be true, after all.

'I'll come to that, Miss Felstead. The whole affair is most unfortunate, and I regret that I have to tell you so soon after your arrival in this country.'

Mr Parker settled back into his black leather chair and continued his explanation. The older Firebraces, he said, had been dead for some time. They left six children, four daughters and two sons. The elder son was a scapegrace, according to gossip, and his father sent him north to Queensland to open up land there. The story went that he was in so much trouble locally that Mr Firebrace senior did this in the hope that the rough frontier life would straighten him out. About two years previously, old Mr Firebrace died quite suddenly, and as he had been a firm believer in the old British principle of primogeniture, the whole estate had passed, to the considerable chagrin of other members of the family, to the eldest child, the older son.

In the meantime, Todd Firebrace had met Edmund Felstead.

'I don't know the whole story, but . . . ' said Mr Parker, almost apologetically, and Amy once again felt that sinking of the heart.

'There were debts, apparently, and Todd handed over the mine and some other property in settlement. Soon afterwards, Mr Todd Firebrace fell from his horse — ahem, he was reputed to be a heavy drinker — and Mr Langdon Firebrace inherited the remaining estate, as Mr Todd had never married and had no issue.'

'And now this Mr Langdon wants that property back?'

Mr Parker smiled, ruefully.

'It is not as simple as that, Miss Felstead. Mr Langdon Firebrace has informed me, through his own solicitors, that another, later, will of his father's has been found, and this later will divides the estate more equably, and that in fact, Mr Todd Firebrace had no right to hand over any of the property to your father.'

Amy turned slightly in her chair, so that she was staring out of the window of this small first-floor office, watching the cabs with their patient horses lined in the rank on the opposite side of the street. How very convenient to find another will, she thought, but she could not bring herself to speak. It was so typical of all her father's enterprises, sounding so splendid, and yet never quite living up to expectation.

'Whether or not this new will can be proven remains to be seen, and in fact, I think we have a good case, as I have amongst your father's papers documents signed by Mr Todd Firebrace acknowledging his indebtedness — gambling, I'm afraid. In addition, your father lost no time in making sure that he had clear title to that property which was handed over in settlement of the debts.'

It sounded like the sort of legal wrangle which could drag on for years, impoverishing all the parties concerned except the lawyers.

'I thought that it took a long time to establish titles to property,' said Amy, mainly because Mr Parker had paused for breath and was fiddling with a pen as if waiting for her

31

to say something. As well, she wanted to drown that feeling of panic. For many weeks, she had pleasurably anticipated moving into, if not wealthy circumstances, some degree of comfort and independence. Instead, she could visualise herself submerged into a sea of legal expenses and endless litigation.

'Not in this country, Miss Felstead. We've adopted the Torrens Real Property Act from our sister colony, South Australia. Transference of freehold real estate is a quick and simple matter.'

'Mr Parker, you must be frank. Was there any purpose in my coming to Australia?'

'Don't give up hope so quickly, Miss Felstead. The Firebrace holdings are quite large enough to absorb the settlement of Todd Firebrace's debts without sustaining any damage. However, from what I hear, Mr Langdon Firebrace is very much a chip off the old block, and his father was said to be a very tough man indeed.'

Amy took a long, deep breath to calm her trembling nerves.

'And the gold-mine? Has that been transferred under this Torrens Act too?'

Mr Parker pursed his lips, fiddled with his pen again, and heaved a great sigh.

'That poses a very pretty problem. The mine was actually worked for a while, but the company operating it was unable to afford the heavy equipment needed to bring up and crush the ore when it was discovered that the lead went deep. Eventually, the company went bankrupt, and the elder Firebrace bought them out for a song, in 1870, just before his death. I don't know what he had in mind, but the mining industry suffered a collapse about that time. Even Ballarat has lost part of its population, and it was our largest and most prosperous gold-mining town. Too many paper companies, Miss Felstead, and not enough production. Well, as you know now, nominally you are the owner of the mine, until the courts decide otherwise, but it is on Firebrace land.'

Nothing in Amy's life had prepared her for all these complexities, but she told herself sternly that just because she was a woman it did not mean that she was incapable of grasping details.

'How can that be?'

'Mining rights are pre-emptive, Miss Felstead. It is rather complicated, I know, for a young lady to understand, but I'll try to make it as simple as possible. When the first claim was taken up on the site of what is now the Royal Edward mine, the land, although leased by the Firebrace family, still belonged to the Crown, which gave miners

33

the right to stake out claims on the said land. Since then, much of the land in the area has become a Firebrace freehold, but gold-mining still takes precedence over other uses. Now, as executors of your father's estate, my firm has taken out a mining licence appertaining to the Royal Edward, and now I wish you to apply for a licence of your own. What it will boil down to, Miss Felstead, is that you have the right to mine, but you will be dependent upon Firebrace goodwill for access to the mine, as it lies entirely within the boundaries of their property.'

'Oh dear.' It was all she could say.

'But you must realise, Miss Felstead, that an enormous amount of capital will be required to bring the mine into production, and if this difficult matter is resolved in your favour, your wisest course would be to sell out to an interested company. On the brighter side, however, the house, which your father occupied prior to his death in the township of Firebrace, was not part of the property handed over by Mr Todd Firebrace. Your father had some capital, and he apparently intended to settle in Firebrace, because he bought the house outright and furnished it. My advice is to either sell the house, or rent it out.'

Amy closed her eyes, trying to raise a

vision of the wisest course to take, and all she could see was money leaking away at a tremendous rate.

'I'm going to Firebrace,' she announced. 'I can live in the house for nothing, and at any rate, I would like at least to *see* my father's mine.'

4

It was a clear, blustery afternoon with a sharp edge to the wind, and Amy was glad of her jacket as she alighted from the coach in Firebrace's main street.

The township, dominated at one end by the scaffolding marking the presence of its sole working mine, was located on a plain sweeping away from the foot of a nearby mountain range, and, being about a thousand feet above sea level, the air here was both crisper and cooler than in low-lying Melbourne. To the south-west jutted another range, jagged and abrupt in outline, and burnished on its bare upper surfaces by the spring sunshine. Firebrace itself was laid out on the orthodox grid lines which comprised standard Australian planning, and was typical of those places which had sprung up as a result of the gold rush. Everything was quite new, and yet already giving the newcomer an impression of being past its prime.

Less than twenty years previously, this land had been part of a huge 'run' leased from the Crown by old Daniel Firebrace for the purpose of depasturage. That is, he could graze animals on the land, but was forbidden by the terms of his lease to practise agriculture beyond his immediate household needs. In those days, Amy would learn from older inhabitants, the plain had been a meadowlike stretch of country, dotted with trees, giving it the aspect of a vast park. The first Firebrace homestead, with its slit windows to give protection against hostile blacks, had been erected on the site of the present newspaper office. It had been burnt to the ground during a wild December night in 1858 when the miners' Christmas celebrations had been interrupted by a bushfire sweeping down from the ranges.

By that time, the Firebrace family had moved to the new homestead, about two miles from the burgeoning town, and were apparently resigned to this invasion of their domain by gold-hungry men numbering thousands at the peak moments of the 'rush'. There had been other rushes in the district, all following the same pattern of a few men, or perhaps one man, finding traces of gold, and then all the hopefuls pouring in, followed closely by blacksmiths, drapers, butchers, usually at least one newspaper operator, gamblers, harlots, goldfields scavengers of every kind, Chinese, and, close behind, a few policemen.

During the next decade, much of the land leased by Daniel Firebrace was resumed by the government, put up for sale, and bought by miners who were hopeful of making a living by farming, although many were ignorant of the skills needed.

So, the land, already stripped of most of its trees by the diggers for firewood, shaft supports, shacks, and every other mining purpose, was put to the plough, whilst the Firebrace family settled down to improving its vastly reduced acreage . . . and waiting. Within a very short time, Daniel Firebrace was able to buy back land from the would-be farmers. Like many another squatter who had been very upset at the changes, he had in fact been enriched by the enlarged market for his meat and soaring wool prices, this latter having been caused by the faraway American Civil War. With plenty of capital, he soon re-acquired the land he had long considered his own.

By 1872, when Amy arrived, the other temporary townships had already vanished, leaving nothing behind but holes and shafts to endanger the unwary, and ugly heaps of clay and stones which would remain barren for many decades. A few old optimists still fossicked about in the ranges, but most of the roving miners had gone too, for the men who worked the Western Consolidated Mine on the outskirts of Firebrace were for the most part Cornishmen, professional miners whose skills in probing deep underground had been handed down since pre-Roman days. This small town also provided a centre for farmers and graziers and all their associated workers.

Standing in the main street, Amy could see that some thought had gone into the planning so that there was a fine view of mountains at either end, but there was little near at hand to inspire the traveller. The standard of architecture was, frankly, poor. Most structures were squat and brown and weatherboarded, with a strange air of impermanence. Some were cottages set back from the street, with the beginnings of gardens in front, while others sat firmly on the edge of unpaved footpaths. The most imposing edifices were the hotels, almost opposite each other, and named, respectively, The Home Rule and The Commercial. One of the passengers on the coach had recommended to Amy that she should seek accommodation at The Home Rule, for The Commercial, as its name implied, catered for men travelling alone, and she could find herself in an uncomfortable situation.

A stout lady in black received her at The

Home Rule. She was the landlord's wife, and despite the Irish-orientated name of the hotel, had a Welsh accent. She scarcely hid her surprise that this pretty young woman was unescorted, and Amy felt obliged to explain.

'I'm Miss Felstead,' she said. 'I've come to Firebrace in order to inspect my late father's property.'

'I'll show you to your room, Miss Felstead,' said the other, after a longish pause. 'You understand that you must receive any male callers in the parlour downstairs?'

Amy felt offended until she realised that this was a standard rule of landladies everywhere, respectable landladies that was. In spite of everything, she thought, with a sudden ruefulness, my life has been too secure, too protected.

The room was small, spartan in the manner of Australian country hotels, and overlooked the main street across the balcony which ran the entire front length of the building. Now that they were in privacy, Mrs Flannagan unbent, but what she had to say was hardly cheering.

'You've come all the way out from the Old Dart, eh? Well, it's a shame you did. There's those who won't be pleased to see you here.'

With that, she nodded her head wisely, and having handed Amy her key, withdrew with a quiet rustle of black poplin.

Conscious that she was trembling a little, Amy began unpacking a few toilet articles, and broke off to go to the window. She did not have direct access to the balcony. That was reached by means of a door at the end of a short passage at right angles to the main hallway upstairs. The sheltering roof and the waist-high fence rather interrupted the view, which was good, overlooking the paddocks stretching away to the heavily wooded country at the base of the mountains to the south-west of the town. Amy was tired after her journey, which had occupied two days, yesterday by train to Ballarat, and today the bone-shaking trip in the coach, but she felt too restless and gripped by curiosity to settle. Sundown was at least two hours away, and acting on an impulse, Amy picked up a shawl, flung it about her shoulders, and went downstairs again.

'Do you know where Mr Felstead's house is?' she enquired of a man who appeared to be employed in the hotel. 'Could I walk there and back before dark?'

'It's just round the next corner, Miss.'

For the second time, she sensed that the mention of the Felstead name aroused a certain speculation.

'Turn to your right when you pass the post office. Next place along is Doctor Jago's place. Then the Felstead house. There's no one there, Miss. It's been empty since Mr Felstead died a few months back.'

'Thank you.'

As Amy stepped briskly along the short, narrow entrance hall, she passed a partly ajar door opening into the main bar. Three men were standing by the counter, and one, directly facing the door, looked at her boldly. He was perhaps in his late twenties or very early thirties, black haired but with the reddish tinge to his smartly barbered whiskers which so often occurs in brunet men of British origin, with piercing dark hazel eyes beneath quizzical brows, a healthily tanned complexion, and a sardonic, almost insolent, half-smile curving his mouth.

The few seconds of their clashing glances sent a throb of annoyance through Amy. A lady-killer, she thought contemptuously. Yes, even here in an out-of-the-way corner like Firebrace, there were men who thought that they had but to leer at a young woman to have her fall helpless at their feet. She lifted her rounded chin resolutely, and fuming because of the ill-luck which had made it appear, just briefly, that she may have *deliberately* looked into that horrid male sanctum, the public bar, she walked with great dignity out into Firebrace's main street.

Amy was not to see her inheritance that day. She had progressed no more than fifty yards towards the corner when a lanky young man of about her own age rushed from behind her, so heedlessly that she was brushed aside, and out on to the muddy roadway, where two tipsy aboriginal men, dirtily clad in ancient cast-offs, stood drinking from a shared bottle.

'You filthy black swine,' yelled the young man, and struck one of the blacks a swinging blow with his left fist.

The unfortunate recipient teetered back, and fell with a thud to the roadway, whilst his companion stared at first in drunken astonishment. Then he recovered himself, and threateningly raised the bottle he held in his right hand.

'Oh, so that's how you want it,' yelled the white man, and, half-crouching, circled the other as if seeking the best spot to land a blow. In the meantime, as Amy, flanked now by two Chinese from the laundry, stared in horror, the other black man scrambled to his feet and lumbered towards the attacker. By this time, a crowd had gathered, including late-afternoon drinkers

43

from the public houses.

'Look out, Jack, he's behind you!' cried out someone, and Jack dodged, with the result that the uplifted bottle, meant for his head, crashed on the cranium of the aboriginal who had already been knocked down.

The bottle broke, and blood and liquor streamed down the victim's face.

'Eh, what's all this?'

The burly figure of a man in the uniform of the Victoria Police pushed its way through the onlookers.

'I'm going to kill them!' shouted the young man called Jack. 'One of their lot killed my brother!' He glared wildly at the crowd. 'You know all about it. I had the letter last week. A filthy black savage killed Bob. My brother. Killed him!'

'Now, Jack,' said the policeman quietly, taking the other gently by the arm, 'you calm down. Old Jim here didn't kill your brother, and neither did Andy. Your brother was killed up near Palmerston,[1] hundreds of miles from here, in the north of South Australia. You know that.'

Another actor moved on to the stage of this drama. It was the handsome man who

---

[1] Palmerston was later renamed Darwin.

had caught Amy's eye with such infuriating boldness.

'Come along, Jack. It's home and bed for you.'

As he spoke, the policeman grinned appreciatively.

'Thank you, Mr Firebrace. Under the circs I don't want to lock Mr Beaton up, but if you'll see to it that he keeps the peace . . .'

Firebrace! That arrogant, insolent man was Mr Firebrace, the very Langdon Firebrace who was trying to snatch away her inheritance! Amy felt another throb of fury. Ogling her as if she were a common shop-girl! Being deferred to by the law as if he were some feudal seigneur, whilst those poor wretched blacks stood there bewildered, one with blood trickling down his broad, ugly nose. Even as Amy's heart almost burst at the sheer unfairness of it all, the injured black man uttered quite the worst obscenities she had ever heard.

'That's enough, ladies present,' snapped the constable, and Mr Firebrace, still gripping Jack Beaton's arm, half turned.

'Go and sober up, the pair of you,' he ordered. 'And I'll expect you tomorrow to start digging out those rabbit burrows. But only if you're sober, understand?'

45

Then he spoke to the policeman in a quiet voice which reached no other ears before moving off with his charge. More Firebrace commands?

'Come along, Andy. I'll take you round to Doctor Jago's so's he can look at that head of yours,' announced the law, quite amiably, before turning to the crowd at large. 'Fun's over. Everyone go home.'

Amy rethought her plans for inspecting the house. Firebrace the town was not as quiet or dull as it had appeared from her hotel bedroom window. Drunken blacks, wild and probably equally drunken young white men were in addition to her own mortal enemy who apparently reigned over the town which carried his own surname.

The following morning, revived by a good night's rest, Amy again set forth to inspect her house. It had rained during the night, and pools of water lay on the unsurfaced main street, providing a hazard for horses and bullock-drawn vehicles, and no less danger for passers-by threatened by splashes of murky red mud. There was patchy sunshine, and a cold south wind which made the girl glad of the jacket she wore over her simple skirt and blouse. She had dressed for practicality today, anticipating that there could be chores to tackle, and also because her experience with Mr Firebrace had instilled in her the suspicion that the motives of a stylishly dressed young woman in a bush town could be misunderstood.

The air was crystal clear, so that the mountains reared bold and blue against the horizon. It seems so strange, she pondered as she walked towards her goal, that all mother's complaints against the Australian climate concerned heat. She often mentioned how hot and tiring it had been, but today is quite as cold as a late-winter day in England.

She turned at the post office corner, after thrusting into the box the letter she had written the previous evening to Cousin Elspeth, assuring that lady of her own safe arrival in Firebrace, and not mentioning the troubles associated with her inheritance. At the end of the letter, she had penned her usual fond regards to Uncle Theo, but had debated for quite some minutes whether or not to pass on good wishes to Charlie Henthorne.

Amy, even at this safe distance, did not wish to encourage Charlie in the smallest way, but neither did she want to hurt his feelings. Charlie, after all, had paid her the great compliment of asking her to be his wife, and it was not his fault that she could not imagine herself in that capacity.

In the end, she did not mention Charlie at all.

Dr Jago's residence was a trim, square, timbered house set back considerably from the street, with a driveway of crushed gravel leading to the front door between two rows of recently planted conifers. A wattle tree, with its early spring glory, which Amy thought of as mimosa, draping its branches, must have been one of the few native trees remaining in the town's yards. Outside the gate, a horse and trap awaited its owner, and she soon perceived that the outfit belonged to the doctor.

A tall man who looked shorter because of his thickset build, with hair verging on the auburn under his hat, hurried out, boots crunching on the fresh-raked gravel, the bag he carried announcing his profession. He almost collided with Amy, and she saw at close quarters a rather tired face, but far from old, with pale grey eyes, pleasant enough, but with something of an habitual impatience marked on it.

'Sorry,' he said. 'If you wish to see me, I've calls to make first.'

Amy smiled, always an exercise which had a soothing effect upon the opposite sex.

'I'm on my way to the next house,' she

explained. If they were to be neighbours, they'd best be on good terms.

'You won't find anyone there.' He paused as he was about to climb up to the seat of the trap. 'The house has been empty for months.'

'I know. But I'm going to live there. I'm Amy Felstead.'

He stared, almost blankly.

'*He* was your father?'

The question was shot at her so abruptly that she was astonished, but he seemed to realise almost immediately that he had been ill-mannered.

'I'm sorry, Miss Felstead. I was surprised. Mr Felstead wasn't a young man. I'd expected Miss Felstead to be — more mature.' He had by now seated himself and taken up the reins. 'I gave medical evidence at the inquest. Do feel free to discuss it with me.'

Then he was off, wheels and hooves sloshing through the mud.

Not a word of sympathy, brooded Amy, watching him leave. Still, I shall speak to him later.

5

The garden of her father's house was surprisingly neat, as if someone had kept the weeds under control, and the boarded floor of the veranda, Amy saw, was free of leaves and other litter which one might have expected to have blown in over several wintry months.

The house was very similar to that of the doctor next door, as if both had been built at the same time, by the same workmen. The design was square, with outer walls of horizontal weatherboards painted pale brown, and the roof was of the corrugated-iron sheets which were fast superseding the wooden shingles or slates of an earlier generation. The dwelling, considering that it had been the home of a gold-fields entrepeneur, was not large, being single-storied, and planned, Amy was able to guess before entering, so that the front door opened directly into a central and fairly wide passage, with rooms placed geometrically on either side, the kitchen and servants' quarters lying across the back.

She was standing before the dark-stained, panelled front door, clutching the key which

50

Mr Parker the solicitor had given her, trying to pluck up the courage to enter, when, with a jerk, the door opened. She uttered a gasp, but surprise was soon allayed by the thoroughly respectable appearance of the neat little woman in her fifties, grey hair pushed up into a white cap, and beady eyes twinkling in anticipation.

'You be Miss Felstead!'

It was not a question, but a statement.

'Yes.' Amy recovered her breath. 'But, who are you?'

'Mrs Arthur Kestle, Miss Felstead.' She had a very strong West Country accent, and Amy had at first to concentrate in order to follow her speech. 'I been cleaning Mr Felstead's house, God rest his soul, as if he'd a been still here. I said to Mrs Morcan Kestle — my sister-in-law she be — someone's bound to come and settle with me one day.'

Amy made a quite mental calculation, balancing out her present meagre assets against several months' cleaning, and probably gardening, and wondered whether a down payment would suit Mrs Arthur Kestle. She also became aware of a quite delicious odour wafting through the house from the kitchen.

'There's the stove and firewood, Miss Felstead. Mr Felstead's stove draws better 'n mine, and I said to Mrs Morcan Kestle, no point in lettin' good wood to waste. Six months' wood, all stacked in Mr Felstead's back yard, asking for snakes to nest in 't, and redback spiders and goodness knows what kind o' bities. So we'll take the wood from the work I've done, and me lad Newlyn in the yard. You can smell Mr Kestle's pasties right now. His dinner when 'e goes down late shift today. He's in Mr Polkinghorne's company at the Western Consolidated. Say what un like, Miss Felstead, where the mine's deep, there's Cornishmen, and Cornishmen need good pasties to keep 'm going. And between 'ee and me, Miss Felstead, my pasties are better 'n Mrs Morcan Kestle's. I say it's th'amount of turnip. She puts in too much.'

Amy had opened her mouth once or twice, vainly trying to find a space through which to break into this intimidating torrent of words.

'Kettle's comin' to boil. When I heard you'd come, Miss Felstead, I said to Mr Kestle, un's bound to come to the house, so I've baked a fresh saffron cake, and the beds are aired. I didn't know what 'ee'd want, Mr Felstead's room, or th'other.'

'I haven't made up my mind.' The girl was floundering. 'I cannot live here on my own.'

52

'Mrs Morcan Kestle's girl Jane'll keep house for you. Quiet, she is. Seventeen last June, but not th'one to be flighty and have followers.'

'Oh dear.'

It was all Amy could utter. She was being borne along by a current of pasties, saffron cake, aired beds, firewood exchanged for housework, and Mrs Morcan Kestle's girl Jane. However, she did seize upon one pertinent fact amidst all the words. News of her arrival had spread throughout Firebrace with astounding rapidity.

While tea was brewing and saffron cake being cut into neat slices, Amy walked through the rooms of the house. They were all as well kept as the outside appearance of the dwelling had promised. The furniture, good without being first-rate, in the dining-room, the parlour, and another apartment used by her father as a study, was dust-free and gleaming with energetically applied polish. Cursorily, she glanced at her father's desk, promising herself that she would check the contents at her leisure.

Until she entered the main bedroom, which had been his, she had little sensation of his presence: it was hard to be sentimental about someone she had not seen for so long, and whom, after all, as she had so often been reminded, had caused her mother much grief.

Her father had slept in a four-poster tester bed, and on the right side stood a table carrying a ruby lustre lamp. To the left, another table top supported several framed pictures. Curiosity drew her to them. There was a photograph of herself as a child of perhaps eight, sitting stiffly in short skirts and white stockings on a carved chair, with a painted drop depicting a painted balustrade to the rear.

'Oh, Papa!' she choked, and the tears, the first she had shed for him, formed under her lids.

Her mother (and was her mother really so strait-laced, as unyielding in life as she appeared here?) occupied another silver frame. This last portrait had been taken, it seemed, at the same time as the one of Amy, judging by the style of the full-skirted dress with white lace collar and matching undersleeves.

There was a framed sketch of her father, made during his American days, for there was a small 'Boston, 1847' written into the bottom left-hand corner. At that time, he had been on the right side of forty, a handsome, dashing man with just the right combination of well-preserved good looks and maturity to capture the heart of an impressionable girl. This was the man who had returned to England, wooed and won her mother against her family's sound advice and wishes, and had carried her off to California and, ultimately, Australia. There was no mistaking Edmund Felstead for anything but the adventurer he had been. In that face, with its high cheekbones, well-defined nose, and large, rather slanting, deep-set eyes, the artist had captured the charm which offset the almost piratical aura which had been so much a part of Amy's father.

There was one more picture on the table, a photograph again, and by the costumes worn by the subjects, who appeared to be in their late teens or early twenties, this was taken about ten years previously. There was no clue to the identity of the young man and woman, although resemblance indicated that they were brother and sister. The legend in the corner was partly obliterated by the heavy frame, but Amy could distinguish the letters 'M-a-t-h' and, beneath that, 'P-h-i-l-a'.

Philadelphia? More America?

The pigeon pair looked familiar, with their strong features, large deep-set eyes, and high cheekbones.

I wonder, Amy thought, whether they are my cousins? Father's nephew and niece?

She knew very little about his side of the family. From Cousin Elspeth and Uncle Theo there had been hints of low origins and disreputable connections, but never had there been any definite references to grandparents, uncle or aunts. Edmund Felstead may well have been an orphan from infancy for all Amy knew about his family. It had always been made clear to her that her mother's marriage had been a misalliance, and any embarrassing in-laws had long ago been swept under the rug of memory and conveniently forgotten.

Obviously, Edmund Felstead had cared for the youth and girl in the photograph, or they would not have occupied a place at his bedside. Amy wished that she knew their names, and she determined to find out whether they had been informed of her father's death.

She promised herself that she would write to Mr Parker in Melbourne, and if he had not already had communication with them, she would search through those of her father's papers remaining in the house in the hope of discovering something about them.

★ ★ ★

She moved into the house that same day. There was no sense, she decided, in wasting precious money on hotel charges when everything was in readiness for her here. With the estate in such a muddled circumstance, and with impending litigation brought about by that horrid Mr Firebrace of the roving eye and arrogant manner, unnecessary expense had to be curtailed. For the first time, she thought seriously of seeking some kind of employment. She was not, as she had expected when she left Britain, a rich heiress, but a young woman who had exchanged the secure semi-servitude of Cousin Elspeth's home for penny-pinching freedom.

Could perhaps she take in a boarder to help with the cost of hiring Mrs Morcam Kestle's girl Jane? Living alone was out of the question, and she needed help to run the house, but however eager Jane might be to enter into her service, she had to be paid and fed. Not that she had had time to make up her mind about Jane — the girl had simply arrived, worn carpetbag of possessions in hand. The Kestles were not a family to let an opportunity pass.

These matters were still very much in her mind when she received Dr Jago in the front room which, however much one would have liked to elevate it to a drawing-room, was still a parlour.

'I took the liberty, Miss Felstead, of calling on you instead of waiting for you to call on me.'

Amy said that this was very kind of him, and seated herself primly on the small sofa by the window. It was five in the afternoon, and the sun, lowering in the sky over the sharp blue outlines of mountains, filtered through the lace curtains behind her to burnish her simply dressed hair. Inwardly, she was glad that Jane Kestle had answered the door. The maid's presence made it clear that Miss Felstead was not alone in the house.

Dr Jago, who had been standing, a little ill at ease, before the newly-lit fire, also sat down. Because he was facing her and the light came from behind Amy, she had the opportunity of studying her neighbour more closely. He was, she judged, about thirty-four or -five years of age, and had the somewhat authoritative air of a professional man. Like many auburn-haired people, he was freckled, the marks on his face being matched by those across the backs of his large, but well-kept, hands. Clean-shaven, he had a strong jaw and a firm mouth, giving credence to her earlier impression that he was a man who liked his own way.

His voice gave force to the idea. It was deep and strong, but a voice which never wasted words, the tone of a medical man who uttered a brief diagnosis and did not expect it to be questioned.

'My condolences, Miss Felstead.'

'Thank you.' She paused, made uneasy by the steady gaze from eyes too light to give much indication of their owner's feelings. 'You said that you could tell me about my father's death.'

'Yes.' From studying her, he changed his target to something vaguely past her left shoulder. 'Sad business. But I'd warned him.'

'Warned him? About the mine, you mean?'

'The mine. None of my business. His heart, Miss Felstead. He was a sick man. Told him to slow up. Any shock could have killed him.'

'But I understood that he died in a rock fall in the Royal Edward mine.'

'So he did, Miss Felstead, but not from the fall. His heart gave out.'

'I see. I could not have understood properly.'

'Mr Felstead was in his sixties. He refused to make allowances.'

Dr Jago was a busy man, and patently eager to leave now that he had fulfilled what he considered to be his duty. Still, he had something further to add.

'Your father had an associate. A man called Samuel McIntyre. Pity he's left the district. He could have told you more about your father's activities.'

He arose, bowed stiffly, and she correspondingly stood.

'I'll see myself out,' he said quickly, and left.

Too late, she regretted not having asked whether he knew the identities of the mysterious pair in the photograph.

* * *

Amy slept in the plainly furnished second bedroom and despite the always pervading Firebrace sound of the crushing plant at the mine on the other side of the township, she slumbered soundly.

She certainly did not hear the unknown person who must have crept quietly on to the veranda only a few feet from her own bed.

6

'Miss Felstead!'

As she cried out, Jane Kestle's rosy face under the thick black hair looked startled, and almost sick.

Amy laid aside the copy of the *Firebrace Gazette*, published three times weekly, which she had been reading whilst drinking her breakfast cup of tea, and realised that Jane had just received a shock.

'It's on the veranda, Miss. I just went out to sweep, like Aunt told me to do first thing so's the leaves and dirt wouldn't blow into the house. It's — oh, it's *nasty*, Miss.'

The front door had been left ajar by the alarmed maidservant, and a very dead animal lay on the door mat, head a mass of congealed gore.

'It's a little wallaby, Miss Felstead. And someone's gone and dumped it right here.'

The policeman, the same man who had intervened when Jack Beaton had assaulted the blacks, listened to Amy's complaint patiently.

'Most likely some silly young buck playin' a practical joke,' he remarked, after inscribing

61

her name and address in his complaints book.

'But why my house? Why should anyone want to do this to me? I moved in only yesterday, and I've been in this town only three days. Three days!'

The constable puckered his lips thoughtfully, and then sighed.

'It's a mite unusual for a young lady to set up house on her own. Unusual for Firebrace, that is.' His tone rather intimated that Firebrace's standards were higher than those of other places. 'It well, don't take offence, Miss Felstead, anyone can see you ain't that sort, but some people have ideas about young women on their own.'

'Oh, they do, do they?' Amy was furious. 'The house belonged to my father, and I inherited it. I have the right to live there, and there is no reason for anyone to object. What about my poor servant? Jane was most upset.'

'That's right. Young Jane Kestle's working for you.' He spoke as if this explained everything. 'One of her admirers who's had 'is nose put out of joint, most like. Get yourself a good watchdog with a loud bark, Miss Felstead. That'll scare any young larrikins away.'

Amy left the police station in a thoughtful

mood. His comments about Jane were contrary to what Mrs Kestle had said about her niece, and made her wonder whether she had been the victim of a confidence trick on Mrs Kestle's part. At the same time, the explanation that the 'joke' had been perpetrated against Jane rather than herself did offer some comfort. Approaching her own gate, she encountered Dr Jago, and she grabbed the opportunity to tell him about the dead animal and ask his advice about acquiring a dog.

'Not everyone liked your father,' he said slowly, and frowned as if going over a list of Edmund Felstead's enemies in his mind. 'But I can't think of anyone who'd take it out on his daughter. A watchdog would be an excellent idea. I'll ask around if anyone 'd be interested in lending you a dog.'

'I'm quite able to afford to buy a dog,' she answered, curtly.

'A loan might be wiser. You'll not be staying in Firebrace very long.'

With this astonishing remark, he touched the brim of his hat, and went on his way before she could reply in protest.

The most annoying part was that what he had said was in all probability true. Why should she stay in Firebrace? The sensible thing to do was to sell the house for what it would fetch and use the money to pay for passage back to Britain. But she would not leave until she had seen the Royal Edward Mine.

She wanted to find out more about the Firebrace family too, and whether conveniently finding a will which had been earlier overlooked fitted in with the general impression of Mr Langdon Firebrace. There was only one way to achieve this aim, and that was to meet people.

In the town there were four hotels: two respectable, in the main street, and two other less presentable establishments elsewhere. To balance up the moral tone, there were four churches, Anglican, small and built of bluestone, the Wesleyan Chapel in proletarian timber, Roman Catholic, half brick and half timber, and most impressive in solid brick, the Presbyterian, for this part of Victoria had been largely pioneered by Scots who had prospered and were generous with endowments. A very small Chinese joss house was never taken into account.

Amy attended the Church of England the next morning, it being Sunday, and slipped inconspicuously into a back pew. Her presence must have been felt rather than seen, for there were little rustles as faces under Sunday bonnets turned for swift glances, and more than one sleekly oiled male head moved fractionally as sharp eyes took in pretty Miss Felstead. A sort of defiance had prompted her to wear her Dolly Varden hat, a flattering piece of silliness which Cousin Elspeth had condemned as outright extravagance.

The parson, a little harassed after a brisk ten-mile ride from his last service, rattled into the preliminaries as if determined to make up for lost time. During the first hymn, Amy caught sight of a tablet set into the wall a few feet away. 'Dedicated to the memory of Letitia Firebrace', the gilt letters said, a perpetual reminder of just who was whom hereabouts.

A late arrival squeezed in alongside Amy. It was Dr Jago, but he did not appear to notice her.

Amy, in her new position, had an angled view through the spaces betwixt bodies, of the occupants of the left-hand front pew. There was Mr Langdon Firebrace, depressingly handsome and prosperous in a dark frock coat, a lady in an elaborate blue bonnet over black curls bunched up behind, and between the pair there was a small and restive child of the female sex. The sight of these people who were set to encompass her financial ruin quite upset Amy's feelings of religious devotion, and lowered still further her opinion of Mr Firebrace. In spite of the bold and consciousless way in which he ogled defenceless and decent young women, he was married, with the evidence right there alongside him.

The clergyman, with the usual keen eye for a new face amidst his congregation, shook her hand warmly as she filed out, and asked her name.

'I'm Amy Felstead,' she said, clearly, very aware that the Firebrace group were only feet away.

'Welcome, Miss Felstead! I do hope that we shall see you again.'

Amy moved out of the small porch into the sunshine, sensible of the atmosphere of hesitancy, a waiting to see which way the cat would jump, amongst the others who were loitering in small conversational groups. Behind her, she heard the parson addressing the Firebrace group with an extra charge of heartiness not offered to the lesser fry.

She was very young, not very experienced, and, suddenly, very much alone. It was all very well to think about showing that she was not afraid, that she did not care if unknown practical jokers flung carrion outside her front door, but the reality of being an object of curiosity was almost overwhelming.

Someone took her arm, gently. It was Dr Jago.

'You must meet some of our good people,' he murmured, brusqueness quite gone, and she felt her gratitude flowing out to him.

A few quick and formal introductions were made, and the fact that she was acceptable to a respected citizen like Dr Jago caused a definite thaw in the coolness of many faces. Regrets were expressed that she had not been able to visit her father before his death, and questions were asked as to how she was enjoying her visit.

How extraordinary. No one expected her to stay.

'Excuse me.' Apparently satisfied that she was occupied, Dr Jago hurried away towards the Firebrace trio, who were now departing after a few formal greetings right and left. At the same time, Langdon Firebrace's eye caught Amy's with a mocking 'You're attractive' expression, which sent an unexpected thrill of excitement through her. Almost immediately, this was suppressed by righteous anger, welling up against this rakish, handsome, powerful man who was so conceited that he flirted openly with young girls within sight of his wife.

'We'd great hopes of the Royal Edward,' one of the town's shopkeepers assured Amy.

'The Western Consolidated won't last for ever, and it'd do a lot for this town if we knew another company was opening up.'

'I don't know very much about it, yet,' Amy had to admit, but at the same time she was observing Dr Jago, who, astonishingly, bent over and kissed the little girl whilst Langdon Firebrace, lighting a thin cigar, watched in amusement. The lady of the family, haughty in her jet-trimmed blue, tightened her mouth impatiently, and made it plain that she wished to be on her way. The Firebraces attended church in style, and now Mr Firebrace assisted her into the carriage, before turning to lift up the child. As the coachman sprung the two horses into action, Langdon turned slightly in his seat, and with absolutely no pretence, scrutinised Amy again, and this time she felt hot colour rising in her cheeks. As the carriage moved off, this near regal exit being a general signal for the dispersal of the rest of the flock, she saw him smile.

'I can offer you a lift,' said Dr Jago, rejoining Amy. 'I have to go out immediately on my rounds, but . . . '

'Thank you, but I can walk. It's a sunny morning, and I'd like the opportunity to see a little more of the town.'

Langdon Firebrace's insolence had upset

her, and, in addition, her confidence in Dr Jago had faded.

'Very well.'

Then she knew that she had to convince Dr Jago that her blush had been brought about by sunshine.

'I'm glad that you didn't introduce me to Mr Firebrace,' she said, recklessly, as she and Dr Jago paused outside the churchyard gate. 'There's a legal action pending between us. My lawyer in Melbourne warned me against holding any kind of conversation with Mr Firebrace or his representatives.'

It was a stupid thing to say, and brought forth an interesting reply.

'If I were you, I'd tell the lawyer to drop the whole thing,' remarked Dr Jago, unhitching his patient horse and removing the nosebag with which the animal had been passing a boring hour. 'Lang's in the right about the mine, no matter what some people in the town would have you believe. McIntyre has a lot to answer for.'

'Mr McIntyre? The man who went away?'

'The same. He had the knack of persuading too many people, including your father. Don't try to fight my brother-in-law, Miss Felstead. You'll end up the worse off.'

She walked homewards in a daze. Instead of finding an ally in Dr Jago, she had made the acquaintance of one who was right in the enemy camp. The disagreeable and rather overdressed Mrs Firebrace must, of course, be Dr Jago's sister. It was like one of those metal tubes containing scraps of coloured glass, the child's toy called a kaleidoscope, with its constantly changing patterns. And what did Dr Jago mean by saying that the mine was worthless?

Was it part of a ploy handed on from Langdon Firebrace to help dissuade her from fighting for her inheritance? Was Dr Jago's warning well-meant or a threat? Her visit to church, meant to establish herself here in the town, had left her confused and more unsettled than before.

7

Loneliness surrounded Amy like a cold fog as she stood on the veranda after her midday meal, staring out across the ragged grass which served as a lawn, over the picket fence, to the vacant paddock opposite, with its mullock heap, the reminder of a brief, furious burst of energy by a hopeful mining team. Beyond that was a straggling line of trees marking the banks of the small river which served Firebrace, and, rearing sawtoothed and imposing in the background, the Grampians. They looked near today, with one or two white clouds hovering on the topmost peaks, and the ravines scoring the granite slopes clearly visible.

The range close to town thrust its less spectacular lower slopes down behind the Western Consolidated's assortment of poppet heads and the buildings which housed the boilers and crushing plant.

Amy, who had plans of her own for the afternoon, had told Jane that she could be free until five o'clock.

'Jane,' she called, going indoors, 'in which direction is the Royal Edward?'

Jane, who had washed and put away the dishes in record time, already had her bonnet upon her head. Remembering those strong hints she had already heard about her servant's flighty ways, Amy suspected that Jane's eagerness to be away was not entirely due to a desire to see her family. The girl's lips looked red, as if she had been biting them, and her eyebrows had been carefully arched by the application of a wet finger.

'It's about two miles out, Miss Felstead,' said Jane casually, with a fervour in her eyes which had nothing to do with mines or their locations. 'If you go to the end of this street, and cut across the Old Police Paddock, you'll see the track going along by Fish Creek.'

'As near as that? I must go there one day,' replied her mistress, airily. Her short stay in Firebrace was rapidly teaching her that it paid to trust no one. What she was likely to gain from her inspection of the mine she could not guess, but she had a vague notion that inspiration would come when she had seen her inheritance.

As soon as Jane had left, she changed into her skirt and jacket, and replaced her soft kid shoes with sensible boots. Then she glanced out at the sky, for the weather in these parts was quite as unreliable as the

72

human population. She decided that the blue was solid enough to be trusted, and slipped out of the front gate after a quick and cautions glance in the direction of Dr Jago's house.

The Old Police Paddock was a piece of waste land which had plainly not been used by the police for a long time. Miners had burrowed in all directions, leaving behind a series of hillocks which had become a rubbish dump and the refuge of a tribe of disgruntled looking goats. Recollecting that male goats had the reputation of being temperamental, Amy scurried nervously along the narrow path to the point where it joined a rather wider track wending alongside Fish Creek, which at this point was more notable for empty bottles than fish.

What this place needs, thought Amy, is a good tidying up, and firmly squashing a few qualms about following the track into the narrow valley, she hurried on, finding herself in an isolated place almost immediately. A fold in the hills cut her off from all sight of the town, and both the track and the creek were confined within the steep walls of a narrow gorge. At intervals, she was amazed to see large burrows dug directly into the loose shale of the hillsides, just large enough to contain a man and his tools, and placing the excavator in constant peril of being buried alive. These were the abandoned efforts of the first wave of miners in the area, those gold-hungry men who had flung aside all sense and caution in their desire for the yellow metal.

A small animal bounded up the hill, a wallaby like the one which had been flung outside Amy's front door, and inside one of the man-made burrows, rock flaked and fell with a startling crack. Half-concealed in new growth at the side of the creek was the rotting remains of a wooden 'cradle', the device used to wash through dirt and rubble dug out by the partner in the tunnel, in the hope of finding 'colour'.

The path became suddenly steeper, and the valley broadened, with the creek veering away from the path, which led now across a wide, almost parklike, stretch of country extending to the base of the first hill. Amy was confronted by a fence, one of the new post-and-wire variety now coming into general use, and a wide wooden gate. 'PLEASE SHUT THE GATE' commanded a painted notice across the top bar, and after a struggle with the piece of hoop iron which kept it in place, she managed to open it, and shut it again behind her.

The hill jutted and reared ahead, and

turning momentarily, she realised that she had been climbing upwards all the way, so that she now looked down across the wide plains which stretched eighty or more miles south to the ocean. The sky to the south was cloudy now, and she tried not to feel uneasy. She was approximately a mile and a half, she calculated, from the township, and the downwards walk should take her no more than half an hour. The Royal Edward must be close at hand. Jane Kestle had said about two miles.

A loud 'baa' made her jump, and three sheep, almost grotesque under the weight of their end-of-winter fleece balanced on four tiny feet, looked at her in that stupid way of their species.

Amy had had a mental picture of her mine, of derricks and boiler-houses and poppet heads and short railway tracks for the trucks. Reality faced her unexpectedly.

There was a boarded-up entrance to a tunnel cut into the hillside, an untidily cleared space before, and the charred remains of a hut standing on a levelled platform of the waste material from the mine. More of this mixture of clay and shale dribbled down into a gully close by, dotted with chunks of quartz, and flattening shrubbery and smothering grass, so that only a few pathetic sticks of acacia thrust up through the mass, trying valiantly to produce a few fluffy yellow blooms.

'KEEP OUT!'

The warning words were painted in large black letters on a piece of whitewashed wood, and nailed across the protective planking at the entrance.

Another notice was held aloft on a post: 'PRIVATE PROPERTY'.

Amy felt very tired, and sat down on a large rock, disappointed beyond belief. This mine, to claim the riches of which she had travelled across the world, was hardly what she had expected.

A yellow-breasted robin bustled about importantly on the ground, while his drab mate busied herself under a tuft of grass nearby. The young woman watched them, and envied them. How simple their lives were, a matter of finding dinner each day and building a nest in season.

Now she saw the wisdom of Dr Jago's advice. There was little point in fighting over this wretched anti-climax of a mine.

But, if it were really so valueless, why did the Firebrace family want it so badly?

If only she knew where the man McIntyre had gone. The more she considered it, the more she was convinced that a conversation with Mr McIntyre would assist her to judge the best course to take. He must know the truth about the worth of the mine. Langdon Firebrace, wealthy and powerful locally, could convince the world that what he claimed was true, that the mine was worthless. It followed that the world would believe, when the other claimant to the mine had been sent upon her way, that new investigations would reveal great riches.

Amy knew next to nothing about mines. She would not have known a piece of gold-bearing quartz from one streaked with iron pyrites, the notorious fool's gold, or cocky's gold, as the Australians called it. However, she was aware that the value of a mine could be judged by an assay made by someone who understood such things. Did her solicitor, Mr Parker, have an assay report regarding the Royal Edward in his possession, or was there such a report amidst those of her father's papers remaining at the house?

She was so engrossed in these thoughts that she did not notice the dog until it barked at her. The animal was a kelpie, the breed favoured as sheep-dog in this country. A prick-eared beast with short, reddish hair and a white chest blaze, it stood in a half-crouching, half-backing attitude, baring its teeth, and generally behaving as if Amy were a dangerous foe.

'Quiet, Tess!'

Without looking about, she knew the owner of that voice, which was British educated, though with a slight Australian twang. The kelpie immediately relaxed, and with a happy 'Aren't-I-clever?' expression, edged past Amy's skirts to join its master.

The girl did not know what to do. She had, she was aware, trespassed on Firebrace property by crossing a small part of it to reach the mine entrance, but at the same time, she was sure that she had the right of access.

'And what are *you* doing here?'

Langdon Firebrace, with Tess panting faithfully at his heels, stared down at her impassively.

'I'm inspecting my property, Mr Firebrace.' She uttered the words sharply, and with an authority she did not feel, at the same time noting that the man had changed from his Sunday best into well-worn garb that was almost shabby.

'*Your* property?' One black, well-marked eyebrow twitched. 'Actually, Miss Felstead — don't be surprised, I know who you are — you are trespassing on mine. I hope you closed the gate behind you? I've had trouble with strangers who haven't observed the first courtesy of country life, shutting the gate after them.'

'I closed your gate,' she retorted. 'I'm not entirely ignorant of your colonial ways, Mr Firebrace.'

She had already learnt, by conversations on board ship, that Victorians, and indeed all Australians, loathed being called colonials, a word which to them had implications of inferiority.

'Well, if you aren't ignorant of country ways, you should know better than to wander about the bush on your own. Apart from the dangers of — um — molestation, Miss Felstead, the country hereabouts is riddled with old mine shafts. You could fall down one and not be found for weeks.'

'I'm not so stupid as to fall down a hole,' she announced, and made to arise, intending to sweep away with a chilling farewell spoken over a disdainful shoulder. To her dismay, she found that her right leg had gone to sleep, and there was nothing for it but to sit again and discreetly twitch her leg under her skirt until the pins and needles subsided.

'When I've made my study of the mine, Mr Firebrace,' she continued, becoming haughtier by the instant, because his quizzical expression unsettled her, 'I shall leave. I must remind you that I've right of way, and can come here any time I choose.'

'There's not much to see, is there?' he remarked, mildly, after a moment or so. He kept looking away, and briefly, she had the suspicion that he was trying hard not to laugh.

'And I should like to know who was responsible for the destruction of the main building!'

Now he did laugh.

'You're being ridiculous,' he said, candidly. 'Main building! That dirty little hut! It burnt down one night last June, and good riddance. Silly old Jimmy and Andy got themselves drunk and let their fire blaze up too high. They were lucky not to be incinerated.'

She now managed to stand upright, determined to put him back into his place, and at the same time very conscious of just how attractive she found him.

'And I should like to know who was responsible for the notices.' She made a grand gesture with one hand.

'I was, of course. This is only a corner of our land, Miss Felstead, but it *is* ours. And I feel a certain responsibility towards those foolish enough to try to explore the tunnel. It's unsafe.'

'You take a great deal of interest in the mine, Mr Firebrace. I had understood that you consider it worthless, not worthy of your Sunday afternoon.'

'Oh, stop it! The mine's a shicer,[1] and don't you think anything else.' Then he laughed again. For such a scoundrel, he did seem a very good-tempered man, more inclined to laugh than to quarrel. 'I was fishing only a few yards away. There's a big pool round the corner of the hill. Tess told me someone was here. Now, Miss Felstead, if you'll come back to the homestead with me, I'll send you safely back to town in the buggy.'

'I shall return as I came, thank you, Mr Firebrace.'

'See those clouds over there? You'll be drenched before you've gone half a mile. And the creek rises very quickly in the ravine. Be sensible and come with me.'

It was all said in that same good-humoured but authoritative tone. Mr Firebrace was apparently so used to having his own way that he seldom had to raise his voice or

---

[1] Shicer — worthless gold claim or mine.

81

display signs of displeasure. Amy glanced up as he talked and saw that a bank of clouds had indeed risen above the horizon and was already obscuring the sun.

'There's a short cut to the homestead up over the hill. It's rather steep, but I'm sure you can manage it.'

Her next words flew out of her mouth before she could prevent them. His galling self-assurance, coupled with his frankly admiring glances, were both too much for her.

'How does Mrs Firebrace react when you bring home stray females, Mr Firebrace?'

This time she did jolt him. He stopped in his tracks, looked her up and down long and hard, and then, infuriatingly, he laughed again.

'Y'know,' he drawled, 'I thought you were one of these new women. All modern ideas and independence. You've disappointed me. I didn't think you'd descend to a trick to find out whether or not I'm married.'

She had never in her entire life felt such a fool.

'Come along,' he added. 'We won't eat you.'

The clouds had grown thicker and blacker, and with visions of the water rising to eddy across the track in the narrow gorge, she followed him. The pool he had mentioned was no more than fifty yards from the mine entrance, and protected by a post-and-wire fence.

'I don't want the sheep falling in,' he explained.

The waters were dark, and placid, fed at one end by a miniature waterfall, and forming at the other a small tributary which joined the main creek a few yards away. What surprised her, however, was that the glen, for such it was, glowed with colour from a dozen varieties of flowering shrub.

'How pretty!' she exclaimed, involuntarily.

'Yes. One of these days, Miss Felstead, I hope you have the opportunity of seeing the flowers over in the Grampian Ranges. They're famous amongst botanists across the world, you know. I haven't met him as yet, but there's a fellow gathering specimens for the Queen's gardens right now. The whole district's been a-buzz over it.'

It was unexpected. One anticipated that a man who conveniently found missing wills and treated his married state lightly would have interests other than botany. Loose living, for example. He was also the first person Amy had met since her arrival who thought that she might stay.

Picking up his creel and rod, he moved

energetically ahead on a path wending up through trees and rocks and more flowering shrubs, steep and quelling to a girl in a bustled skirt and a tight jacket over stays and petticoats.

Tess, panting, bounded ahead, pausing at the first turn as if to enquire what was delaying those lazy humans. Determined to make a good showing, Amy struggled after the man, coping as best she could with the slippery places and spots where footholds had to be chosen with care. Nearly at the top, she reached for a sapling overhanging the path to steady herself, and then paused, frozen momentarily as waves of giddiness flooded through her. The plump St Andrew's Cross spider which had been poised in a web mere inches from her hand withdrew hastily, and dizzily Amy tried to regain control of herself. How stupid was this phobia of hers, how childish, and how impossible to overcome.

'Come along,' called out Mr Firebrace, reaching over and taking her hand, 'the worst is nearly over.'

Out of the corner of her eye, she looked down and saw that at this point the drop was almost perpendicular, straight down into the pool, above the little waterfall. The man's grip remained strong and unfailing, and in another second she was at his side on the summit.

'Now, what was wrong with you? You went as white as a sheet. Can't you stand heights?'

'I nearly put my hand on a spider. I know it's absolutely silly of me, but they upset me terribly.'

'My sister Allison's like that about cats. I'd rather have a cat in the house than be forever risking my fingers or toes in mousetraps, but she won't abide one.' He did not seem to think Amy's peculiarity strange, or the butt of teasing as did Cousin Elspeth. 'Don't care much for spiders myself. A redback nipped me when I was about fourteen and I was sick for days. During my school holidays, too.'

The slope on the other side of the hill was much gentler, and she could see the homestead, set in a quite spacious garden, apart from the usual outbuildings of a big farm. The sky was imminently threatening a deluge, and she had to run to keep up with his long stride.

'By the way,' he said, as they reached the gate leading into the homestead garden, 'I'm single. My sister housekeeps for me. Little Avis is our niece. My next sister one up married Eric Jago. She died when Avis was born.'

So there it was. Langdon Firebrace, her opponent in the battle for possession of the Royal Edward, was single, and Amy wished heartily that he had been married, fifty, fat, and the father of ten children.

8

Nothing was as it seemed, or should have been. Even Jack Beaton, who drove her home, and who was that same wild young man who had attacked two blacks in Firebrace's main street, was now revealed as a shy yokel with little to say.

This silence gave Amy time to think as the buggy jogged downhill towards the township. Mr Parker's information that the Firebrace family lived in a veritable mansion was incorrect. The homestead was a large and comfortable house, nothing more.

Langdon Firebrace, who had given her the unfortunate first impression of being a man with scant respect for women, was, on closer acquaintance, a rather jolly and down-to-earth person.

But there were other aspects of her afternoon's adventures which were more disturbing. One was that Miss Firebrace was cold and unfriendly. Her brother might seek to disarm Amy with a friendliness which ignored her first rebuffs, but Allison did not bother to dissemble. Just as vexing was that glimpse of the parlourmaid, a rosy-cheeked brunette so like Jane Kestle in appearance that for a moment Amy had thought the girl to be her own servant.

Nearing home, she remarked on the resemblance to Jack Beaton.

'That's Mary Anne Kestle,' he replied. 'Jane's sister.' Then, spoken fiercely, as if torn from the heart of a young man who, sober, was quiet and self-effacing, came the bitter question. 'Jane, she's got a new suitor, ain't she?'

For Jack Beaton to even utter such things revealed the extreme of hurt and jealousy to which Jane had driven him.

'I know very little about Jane.'

What Amy did know was that she wished she had not been so easily inveigled into employing Jane Kestle. She saw clearly the wisdom of Cousin Elspeth's absolute insistence on well-substantiated references when hiring servants. Jane was not only flighty, but there was the possibility that she had been introduced into Amy's house for a purpose. Had the idea that Jane would make an excellent servant for the newcomer been planted in Mrs Arthur Kestle's head?

She recorded the day's events in her diary.

'Went to church. Afternoon, investigated mine. Little to see. Encountered Mr Firebrace. Quite amiable. (Is this a pretence?) Met Miss

Firebrace. Came home in F. buggy. Must do something about J.K.'

★ ★ ★

She slept for a while, but was aroused after midnight by the noise from Western Consolidated as the donkey engines started up again after the silence of the Sabbath. Amy began thinking in that urgent, intense way of the pre-dawn. Should I sell this house, stop worrying about the rest of the estate, and find a suitable position as governess or companion?

This was her rational half trying to make the best of things. The other part, the other Amy who was too like her father for her own good, the girl who had tossed away dull security and the chance of a fairly good marriage for the sake of a will-o'-the-wisp fortune, shot off at a tangent and had to be pulled back severely.

Mr Firebrace was not married. He had made a most peculiar remark to the effect that she would still be in Firebrace in the future to travel to the Grampians and . . .

Oh, stuff! Back to common sense and hard thinking.

If only she could talk with Mr McIntyre.

And what about the wills, especially the

new one which had turned up so very conveniently?

She did fall asleep again, to be awakened sharply by the combined din of the Western Consolidated steam whistle, a whole clan of magpies carolling to one another, and two laughing jackasses intent on deafening out the opposition. As happens when one has done some hard thinking during the night, Amy felt tired and dull, and when Jane handed her the envelope after breakfast, she looked at it uncomprehendingly.

'Found it on top o' the gatepost, with a stone top 'f it,' said Jane, bustling off towards the kitchen.

The legend, 'MISS AMY FELSTEAD', stared up at Amy in coarse letters which had been painstakingly cut from a printed sheet. The one piece of paper inside, cheap and unsized, carried only four words, still in those same printed letters, not all in the same case, but as large as could be easily found:

'GET OUT OF FIREBRACE.'

After the first shock, anger flowed through her, the crusading anger one feels only when young, lending intensity to purpose, and not stopping to weigh pros and cons.

'Look at that!' she cried, catching up with the startled Jane, 'So! How abominable!'

'Awful,' whispered Jane, withdrawing a

little. 'Who'd do a thing like that, Miss Felstead?'

'The same person who threw that dead animal on my doorstep! It couldn't be anyone else!'

That mutilated creature had been meant for her, not for Jane, as Constable Price the policeman had suggested. This letter proved it.

What to do first?

This time, she did not go to the police station. Instead, she went to the office of the township's newspaper.

The *Gazette* came out three times weekly, not attempting to compete with the Melbourne dailies which arrived regularly on the coach, but filling up with small local items of news, and advertisements. Job printing provided a large part of the business, and any dodgers distributed in the district, either to advertise sales, visiting entertainments, or suchlike, were almost sure to have originated from the *Gazette* office.

A youngish man in a leather apron was working the noisy press in the back room as Amy entered the front part of the *Gazette* building, which was of two rooms, weatherboarded, and single-storied. Oscar Howarth, the owner-editor-cum-feature-writer, busy with scissors and paste as he prepared part of the next issue of the *Gazette,* glanced up and reflected pleasure as he perceived the prettiness of his visitor.

'Would this print,' demanded Amy, coming straight to the point, 'have come from your paper?'

Howarth took the sheet from her, pursing his lips and then putting it down briskly.

'Cut from our dodgers, I'd say,' he remarked. 'What's this about, young lady?'

'My name is Amy Felstead. That was left on my gatepost.'

'Felstead? You're Edmund's daughter, then.' The other, fortyish, balding, and with the enlarged veins which came from many years of assiduous drinking, absolutely beamed. 'I'm Oscar Howarth. Glad to meet you. I heard you'd arrived and moved into your father's house. Mind if I put an item in the paper about it? Will you be staying long, and that sort of thing.'

'Someone doesn't want me to stay,' she answered, indicating the anonymous message.

'There are some odd people about, Miss Felstead. The kind who think a young lady on her own is fair game. Take my advice, and go to the police about this. It's someone who lives hereabouts, that's obvious. Any ideas of your own?'

'No.' Suspicion and instinct were one thing, direct evidence another.

'Worrying.' He scribbled a few notes on a scrap of paper. 'Thinking of working the mine, Miss Felstead?'

'There seems to be some doubt about the position,' she replied, cautiously. Then, realising that the other had used her father's given name and must have known him fairly well, she plunged in with a direct question. 'What did my father think of the mine, Mr Howarth?'

Howarth frowned, and fiddled with his pencil.

'I don't rightly know. It was all very much in the early stages. And young Lang Firebrace was up in arms about it. But there's a lot of people round here who'd like to see the Royal Edward worked. It would keep things moving here in town. The Consolidated won't last for ever.'

'Why should Mr Firebrace be so against the mine reopening?'

Mr Firebrace had told her that the mine was worthless, but she saw no reason to believe him.

Howarth scratched at his thinning hair with the end of his pencil.

'Could be any one of a number of reasons. It might be sheer contrariness. The mine re-opening would mean having to allow access. Or sour grapes because it slipped out of his fingers. Then the springs which supply his homestead with water rise in that hill. Gold-mines need water, and plenty of it, Miss Felstead, to wash through the crushings so's the gold'll drop out. There's another reason, too, Miss Felstead.'

He paused, as if not altogether willing to say more.

'Mr Howarth,' she said, a little desperately, 'I came from England because I thought I'd inherited a fortune. Now I'm faced with a law suit over what I expected to be mine.'

Howarth, unexpectedly, grinned.

'So he's going ahead with it. Well, it fits. He's a squatter, after all, and a man has to be in a big way to do well out of sheep these days. He's been carrying on from where his father left off, quietly buying up the land from the selectors . . . '

'Excuse me, Mr Howarth, but you'll have to explain what is meant by a selector.'

'A selector is a small farmer, Miss Felstead, allowed to take up an area of Crown land and pay it off over a period of time, direct to the government. A lot of the men who came out here to try mining thought they'd make farmers, but they didn't know the first thing about it, and wore out the soil after two years. The land was so cheap that they still make a profit selling out at three pounds an acre.'

'But how can that affect the Royal Edward?'

'Simple. If the mine is worked, more people'll come out here to Firebrace. We'll most likely get the railway. Then the couple of farmers who've clung on close to town could sell off their land as town blocks instead of letting Mr Firebrace buy it up for grazing, much more cheaply.'

'I see.' Amy had had scant commercial experience, but she understood arithmetic. If Langdon Firebrace bought up that land cheaply, he stood to gain either way. Should the Royal Edward remain unworked, he would have his extra grazing land, and if the reverse happened, he would do very well by selling off that same land for building sites. It was, therefore, in his interest to have people believe that the Royal Edward was valueless.

'But I'll tell you now, Lang isn't the sort to resort to cheap tricks like this.' Howarth held up the letter. 'He's as hard and tough as his old father, for all that he's enough charm to soothe a tiger snake in a rage. But that's not his style. Why should it be? He's a rich man, and as far as this district goes, the Firebraces are top dogs.'

Amy would dearly have loved to discuss the Firebraces further, but intuition bade her caution. What was it Cousin Elspeth had said? If a person tells you a lot about a third party, you can be sure that he discusses *you* with others. On the other hand, Mr Howarth was obviously a source of local information, and he had known her father fairly well.

'Mr Howarth,' she said, 'did my father ever mention his American connections to you? I think that I may have relatives in the United States. Mr Parker, the solicitor, did not mention them, but there is a picture at the house of two people I think may be my cousins.'

'H'm.' Howarth pondered. 'I didn't know Edmund as well as all that.'

'My father must have done quite well in Queensland.'

'Yes. Well enough, from what he said. He'd made up his mind to settle here. I suppose you were preparing to come out when you heard he'd died.'

'Come out?' Amy's voice faltered in her surprise.

'Yes. That's what I understood. He'd written to you.'

'Yes, of course.' She did not want to betray the puzzlement she felt. She had received no letter. Had it been delayed? Or gone astray? Even in these modern times, ships foundered, with the loss of all cargo and mail aboard.

At the same time, she had to fight back the suspicion that Elspeth, her heart set on Amy's marriage to Charles Henthorne, had quietly taken and destroyed any letter with a Victorian stamp which might have arrived.

Yet, there was through her a warmth. Her father had wanted her to come. He had intended that she should make her home here in Firebrace. Well, whatever happened, it would take more than a few stupid practical jokes to scare her now.

With this new strength of purpose, she had no hesitation in confronting Dr Jago as he returned home from his afternoon rounds. He looked tired, and hardly in the mood for idle talk with his pretty young neighbour, but Amy was determined. If the odious Mr Langdon Firebrace were indeed behind these nasty little japes, the best way to let him know that she was undismayed was through his brother-in-law.

'Dr Jago,' she demanded, thrusting the sheet of paper at him, 'do you know whether anyone else has received one of these?'

He stared down at it, frowned, and then

examined the missive again.

'Get rid of the Kestle girl,' he snapped. 'Plainly meant for her!'

'The envelope was addressed to me.'

'This is a matter for the police,' he declared, reddish brows drawing together in annoyance. 'A crank sent this, and, Miss Felstead, you shouldn't treat these things lightly.'

'Who were my father's enemies, Dr Jago?'

The question hovered, while he did not quite meet her eyes with his own.

'You shouldn't let your imagination run away with you,' he replied, after a lapse of several moments. 'I'll keep my ears open. You're probably not the only one who has received one of these stupid notes. But you do need a watchdog.'

This seemed to end the conversation, but as he turned to go, he apparently remembered something else.

'Miss Felstead, are you by any chance interested in taking up teaching? The young woman who was assisting Mrs Stacey at Mrs Stacey's private school is leaving the district at the end of the week to be married in Melbourne.'

'Why . . . Thank you! I'll enquire tomorrow morning.'

It had been a quite fruitful day.

9

That same evening, Amy settled down to the task of sorting through those papers of her father's which had been left in his desk. She had two particular aims in mind: to find out something about her father's American relatives, and to seek a clue as to the whereabouts of the elusive McIntyre.

Those papers which had been left by Mr Parker's clerk were disappointingly meagre. There was no address book, and Amy resolved to write to Mr Parker and enquire whether any such had been taken with the other papers. Neither was there any lead as to the identity or whereabouts of the American duo, but as she replaced the bundle of papers in the desk, she saw something she had missed earlier. A careless, scrawled signature across the bottom of a receipted account from a firm of Ballarat mining consultants read 'S. McIntyre'.

There was an address on the letterhead, and without hesitation, she sat down and penned a brief request that Mr McIntyre contact her as she wished to discuss matters pertaining to her father's mine, the Royal Edward.

This done, the girl sat near the lamp, unwilling to admit to herself that she was deliberately delaying the moment when she would finally turn down the lamp before climbing into bed. Jane Kestle's door had closed an hour before, and Amy, mind no longer occupied, found herself straining to hear any strange sound which might superimpose itself on the quiet and persistent thud of the machinery at the Western Consolidated on the other side of the town.

I'm silly, she told herself, resolutely. The house is securely locked. I must go to bed and sleep soundly, because I need to be at my best tomorrow morning when I am interviewed about the position at the school.

In spite of this resolution, she did lie for some time in a nervous wakefulness. About midnight, she heard Dr Jago driving in from a late call, and this was comforting. His return would surely have scared off any would-be prankster, and she fell asleep quite suddenly.

After a brief conversation, Mrs Stacey suggested that Amy spend the rest of the day helping at the school, this being the practical way of assessing her suitability. At the end of the day, Mrs Stacey told her that she could consider herself engaged as assistant. The remuneration must necessarily be small, but Amy, knowing that this was as good a job as she could hope to find, accepted readily. The alternative was to dismiss her servant and live alone.

On the way home, somewhat worn after her first day with numerous small children, she met Constable Price face to face.

'You should have brought that letter to the station, Miss Felstead. I'd be obliged if you'd leave it when you happen to be passing. Nasty sort of mind behind it.'

News in this small town was never static. It travelled from person to person with astonishing speed.

Rebuked, she continued on her way, trying to ignore the ribald remarks emanating from a group of tipsy shearers gathered outside one of the less respectable hotels. The annual ritual of harvesting wool was almost completed in the district, and most of the sheep, so superior and top-heavy but a fortnight since, were now shorn down to the ridiculous appearance of being publicly caught in their underwear.

'You should know better than to walk past here on a pay day,' said a voice in her ear, that already well-known voice which had the most alarming effect upon Amy's equilibrium.

Langdon Firebrace, dressed neatly but casually in his workaday uniform of riding clothes, fell into step alongside, and the offensive remarks ceased immediately.

Having protected her from the coarseness of the shearers' remarks, he did not, as she expected, move away on his own business, but lingered. His sister, he said, was shopping, and he would have to wait for her. He asked Amy how she was finding life in an out-of-the-way bush town, and expressed genuine interest when she told him that she was now Mrs Stacey's assistant.

Amy, who, in imagined encounters with Langdon Firebrace, was always mistress of herself and able to crush him with well-chosen remarks, stood there meekly, answering his questions, and trying to quell the fluttering sensation behind the buttons of her jacket.

Little Avis, he told her, would very likely attend Mrs Stacey's school the following year, it being understood that the child would then return to her father's care here in town. Her expression showed her mystification, and he enlarged.

'My sister Anne died two weeks after Avis was born. Poor Eric — Dr Jago — went very much to pieces, and it seemed sensible at the time for Allison to take over caring for the baby.' Then, abruptly, he changed the subject. 'We can't talk out our problems here in the street, Miss Felstead. Could I possibly call on you, Sunday afternoon perhaps, so that we can discuss what's best to do?'

The euphoria which had so treacherously wrapped itself about Amy evaporated. Pleasant social chit-chat was replaced by the reality of her position.

'Our problems, as you call them, are in the hands of my solicitor,' she answered.

'You're being foolish. We could sort out the whole thing in an hour.'

'To your advantage, I'm sure!' The retort came out hot and bitter, and she walked away, seeing, out of the corner of her eye, Miss Allison Firebrace bearing down upon her brother. The frown on her features demonstrated that, however much Langdon Firebrace employed his charm to undermine Amy, Allison's methods were much more direct.

It was a relief to be inside her own front door, to pull off her gloves and place slightly shaking hands against hot cheeks. I am not, she told herself sternly, a silly dithering damsel in a romance. I am a girl of today, quite in control of myself, and well able to manage my own affairs. I shall not be swayed by challenging hazel eyes, nor a deep voice tinged with humour, nor mere good looks. My mother fell into that sort of trap.

This last thought brought her up with another jerk. Marriage had been the end result of the fatal attraction her father had exercised over her mother. Mr Firebrace was endeavouring to soften her feelings towards him so that he could obtain full possession of the Royal Edward.

The meal served up by Jane Kestle was only fair, and Amy's mind turned to Dr Jago's advice to find lodgings. Settled with a good landlady, she would be far better off in all ways, but leaving her house now would convince that anonymous practical joker that he had won.

Unsettled, but resolute, she lit the lamp in her father's study, and examined the books on the shelves. Having become a teacher, she needed to polish up the lessons of her own childhood. Novels by Messrs. Dickens and Trollope were unlikely to be of much practical aid, but there was an atlas, and she tackled this with some determination.

Raising her gaze, momentarily, she glimpsed something which worried her so much that she put aside the atlas and crossed to her father's desk. A white corner of paper protruded, caught as the top of the desk had been closed.

She was a naturally tidy person, and positive that all inside had been arranged neatly when she had finished there the previous night. The key was still in the lock, where it had been when she had arrived in the house for the first time. There were no secrets nor valuables in her father's desk, and no reason for keeping the key elsewhere.

She pulled down the top, and saw indisputable evidence that the desk had been searched that day. It was not exactly untidy, but neither was anything back in its original place.

Amy took the lamp and went into her bedroom. Now, she said to herself, we shall see just how thorough this person was. She climbed on to the seat of a chair, and felt behind the ornamental top edging of the heavy wardrobe. The packet of correspondence which had passed between her and Mr Parker, including copies of her own replies, lay in precisely the spot where she had placed it. As well, the heavy, rounded pebble which weighed down the packet was, she was sure, untouched.

I did not, she thought, with some satisfaction, as she lowered herself from the chair, come down in the last shower of rain.

She returned to the study with the lamp, and then called out to Jane Kestle.

'Jane,' she said, quite pleasantly, 'were you in all day today?'

Jane's gaze met hers boldly at first, and then moved shiftily.

'Yes,' she muttered, making a pretence of wiping her hands on her apron.

'Someone has been interfering with this desk. Was it you, Jane?'

'No, Miss. I didn't touch it, honest I didn't.' Jane was straining to convince her, and then she decided that perhaps honesty was best. 'I did go out, Miss. Only for half an hour. I slipped round to my aunt's. Uncle Arthur's been sick. They're scared it's the miners' disease. He's been coughing something awful.'

'I'm sorry to hear that. Did you lock up carefully, Jane?'

'Oh, I think so, Miss.' Jane was now eager to make amends. 'I won't do it again, Miss. It's just that I've been worried about Uncle Arthur. They've been good to me. Better'n my own.'

It was the first hint Amy had had that all was not well between Jane Kestle and her parents. She decided to follow it up when the opportunity availed.

'All right, Jane. Whoever it was didn't

take anything. There was nothing to take, in any case.'

Little liar, she thought, as Jane, anxious to please, scurried off to make cocoa. She *knows*.

Yet, all the while, Amy did not really want to accept the only logical explanation. Langdon Firebrace had been in town that afternoon. Had Jane been telling the truth when she said that she had slipped out for a while? Had the intruder, seeing the servant returning, pushed papers back carelessly before escaping? If Jane had been the culprit, it was unlikely that she would have been so stupid as to leave the desk in a state which advertised that an unauthorised person had been rifling through the contents.

Amy drank the cocoa and nibbled a biscuit. She would not let the matter rest, but there was no point in pushing it further tonight. Jane had been alerted, and needed to be taken unawares.

The next morning, after peeping outside to check on the weather and deciding to take her umbrella, Amy carried through this decision. The school was only a few minutes' walk away, and she had allowed herself ample time. Quite casually, she remarked that Jane had an admirer in Jack Beaton. Cousin Elspeth would have disapproved of such familiarity, but Amy doubted whether her relative had ever found herself in similar circumstances.

'Oh, him,' shrugged Jane, who was dusting with her usual assiduity, for, to give her credit, she was a good housekeeper. 'I've someone better now. Jack's gone a bit touched since his brother got killed. Speared 'e was by blackfellows while 'e was workin' on th' Overland Telegraph. Jack's full of talk 'bout going north and revenging himself, but that's all it is, talk.'

'You should be careful, Jane. Jack Beaton is angry over the way you've treated him.'

Jane moved her body in a fashion reminiscent of a satisfied cat.

'It's like I said. I've found someone better. It was all over with Jack before I went to Ballarat.'

'Oh?'

'Yes. I was working as a chambermaid in a pub there for a bit. Then I come back.'

Amy surmised that Jane Kestle had been fired, perhaps without a reference, which explained why her aunt was so eager for her to enter Miss Falstead's service. And how much Firebrace connivance was involved?

'My new friend's a proper gent.'

As Jane spoke, there was something of contempt in her voice. She, the servant, had lovers. Amy, the mistress, had none.

'Well, I don't want your followers calling at the house,' snapped Amy, irritated at having it made so plain that she was a failure in Jane's estimation. 'Now I must be on my way.'

Sheltering under her umbrella in the fine, driving rain, she strode along with as much vigour as her skirts allowed, trying to work off her anger and the monstrous suspicion which made her heart pump with the emotion it generated. So Jane's new lover was a 'proper gent', was he?

Mr Firebrace, for instance?

Several days slid by, marked only by three events of any significance. The first was the arrival of the watchdog, delivered by Dr Jago. It was a tan-coloured kelpie, so similar in appearance to Langdon Firebrace's Tess that Amy instantly remarked upon it.

'It's from the same litter,' admitted Dr Jago, fixing her with that light, opaque stare of his, as if daring her to argue. 'He's no good as a sheepdog, but Miss Firebrace assured me that he's an excellent watchdog. She thinks that I needed him myself, by the way.'

Now, what was she to make of that? Mac made himself at home without much ado, and although Jane Kestle complained that

109

she did not want a dog under her feet, Amy allowed him to stay. A show of compliance, she reasoned, might cause certain persons to over-reach themselves.

A second occurrence was afternoon tea with her new employer, Mrs Stacey, on Saturday. That good lady would have been horrified if anyone had accused her of being a gossip. She considered herself quite above the purveyance of tittle-tattle, but she was something of a snob, and loved talking about the district's better people, who were, in her opinion, those members of the older pioneering families who still lived within twenty miles of Firebrace. She looked down on the mining community, although the young daughters of the more affluent were amongst her paying pupils. Amy, demurely sipping tea, remarked that Mr Langdon Firebrace had told her that the little girl, Avis Jago, might be attending the school the following year.

'Ah, yes.' Mrs Stacey uttered a sigh, and the big cameo brooch on her bosom rose and fell. 'Dr Jago wishes it, but Miss Allison prefers that the child be taught at home.' Her voice became wistful. 'A very sad situation. Such a *fine* family, but then, these difficult situations can arise in the best circles. The eldest girl married extremely well, you know.

A baronet with a seat in Buckinghamshire. And the second one did nearly as splendidly. One of the *top* families in New South Wales. A land grant back in 1808. But there's been so much tragedy in such a short time. Poor Miss Anne who married Dr Jago, then old Mr Firebrace, and Mr Todd Firebrace. Miss Allison seemed to be in mourning forever.'

'Dr Jago must have been sad, too.'

'Oh, Dr Jago.' Mrs Stacey spoke in the manner of one who, having been recalled from the Elysian Fields, has to make do with the commonplace. 'A fine doctor. Not that I've had a day's illness in years, the Lord be thanked. But, no money of his own. Old Mr Firebrace was against the match, but Miss Anne would not be denied. Of course, it was Miss Allison he courted first. Miss Anne was fresh home from visiting her sister in England, and she snatched Dr Jago from under Miss Allison's nose. They were married just eleven months when Miss Anne died. Miss Allison took the child and . . . A very sad affair. One cannot help wondering how it will end. Sooner or later, Mr Langdon Firebrace will decide to marry, and Miss Allison's position will be very different.'

'Oh, Mr Firebrace is engaged, then?' The question slipped out quite naturally, giving no hint of Amy's fierce interest.

'Well . . . ' Mrs Stacey's lips pursed. Her visitor was young, single, and her employee, but the older woman always had difficulty in keeping things to herself. 'No, not engaged. But there is an attachment. A woman in Ballarat. She is separated from her husband. There's no future in it, but sooner or later Mr Firebrace will realise that he has an obligation to marry to carry on the name.'

It sent Amy home in a strangely melancholy frame of mind, and when, the following morning, a certain dark head immediately swivelled about and a smile was flashed in her direction as she entered the church, she pretended not to notice. Mrs Stacey referred to the lady in Ballarat, delicately, as an attachment, but what she meant was a mistress. Men did not travel all the way to Ballarat over atrocious roads merely to sip tea. And Jane Kestle had been in Ballarat until recently.

If only the wretched man were not so attractive!

Afterwards, she nodded briefly at persons with whom she had become acquainted, intending to bolt homewards, but there was to be no escape.

'Good morning!'

There he was, right in her path, smiling down at her quizzically, while she had to raise a hand to still her Dolly Varden hat, which was straining a little in the breeze.

'Good morning, Mr Firebrace.'

'May I call on you this afternoon?'

'I must remind you, Mr Firebrace, that I live on my own, with only a servant for company. I have my reputation to consider.'

He seemed taken aback.

'I wanted to talk to you privately.'

'I made it plain the other day, Mr Firebrace, that any — any exchange between us must be through our lawyers.'

'My sister is indisposed today, otherwise I'd insist that you come home with us for dinner. *That* would overcome all this rubbishy business about your reputation.'

She was painfully conscious that the rest of the congregation was passing them, observing this tête-à-tête and no doubt assessing its worth as material for future gossip.

'You must excuse me.'

She hurried home, realising that she had never been so utterly miserable in her entire life.

This, then, was the third in the minor sequence of events which would later be seen as the preliminary to the main drama.

10

A quiet week slipped by, and on Friday afternoon, a little later than usual because she had stopped in the main street to do some shopping, the tired new school assistant paused before her front gate. The children had been exuberant all day, and her own shortcomings as a teacher shown up on several occasions, and it was with half-thinking curiosity that she picked up the small cardboard box on her gatepost and opened it.

A large, hairy and brown-coloured spider leapt out and scurried across the back of her hand to make a flying jump on to the gatepost and freedom.

The scream in her throat could not emerge. She felt hot, cold, and hot again, while the world swum about her.

A voice, a strange, feminine voice, with an odd accent, came to her from the mists.

'What's wrong, honey? You not feeling well?'

A slim black hand was on her arm, a white face was peering into her own.

Amy fainted.

'Nothing much wrong. A simple faint. Miss Felstead has been under strain lately.'

She lay on the sofa in the little parlour, which seemed crowded with three people who stood watching her with some concern.

There was Dr Jago, impassive of expression as usual, a coloured woman of negro origin, so much an oddity in this part of the world that she seemed part of a dream, and a tall, slender white woman, elegantly dressed in tobacco-coloured silk trimmed with black jet and fringe.

'You're fine now, honey.' The white stranger approached, and her well-curved mouth widened into a smile.

She was quite familiar to Amy, but the girl knew that they had never before met. She was about thirty years of age, and her features had lost the prettiness of first youth, having settled into handsomeness reflecting a strong personality. The hair, dressed with skilled fingers into a style of some sophistication, was of the same chestnut as Amy's, yet the face had a faintly olive cast, with slightly slanted dark eyes set above high cheekbones.

'I'm your half-sister, Hannah Felstead.'

The words passed by Amy, for these were creatures in a dream, and the only solid reality was Dr Jago.

'I'm sorry to have been so foolish.'

'Standing all day in tight lacing, no doubt,' said Dr Jago, and then he glanced towards the handsome lady in tobacco-brown silk. 'I'll leave her in your care.'

Having delegated responsibility, he left, and the woman who claimed to be Hannah Felstead spoke again.

'Polly, go tell the maid to brew some tea. We'll take it in here.'

The negro woman left, a plump yet supple creature nearly as well turned out as her mistress, who now seated herself gracefully.

'You must be very surprised,' she said, to the dazed Amy.

'You're the girl in the picture in my father's bedroom.'

'Thank you for recognising me. That picture must be more than ten years old.' Hannah reached out her right hand, embellished by an enormous topaz ring, and placed it on Amy's arm. 'We arrived on the coach not an hour ago, honey, with our bones almost shaken out of our bodies. And it seems that we arrived just in time.' She cocked her head to one side, regarding the younger woman critically. 'You've let yourself run down, have you, honey?'

'Someone played a joke on me!' Amy

116

sat up, fighting faintness, but determined to overcome it. 'There was a little box on the gatepost, and I picked it up, and the most horrible spider jumped out. It was like everything else which has happened. Someone wants me to leave Firebrace!'

'I didn't see a spider, but there was a little box lying on the ground, I think. Polly and I just grabbed you, and, fortunately, the doctor next door was driving along the street, and he came in with us.'

Polly came in, bearing a tray with tea things, and she set it down, at the same time glancing towards Hannah Felstead. Her mistress seemed to understand what was in her mind.

'I'll call you in a few minutes, Polly. First, I must talk with Miss Felstead.'

She took over the pouring of the tea, and, fleetingly, Amy was reminded of Cousin Elspeth, who always assumed command, even to, she suspected, quietly pirating letters which could upset her plans.

'Considering that our father was a goldfields tycoon, he didn't live in any very grand style,' Hannah commented, with a shrug. 'I'd expected something much larger.'

'The house is mine. It was left to me. I'm sorry, but I didn't even know of your existence — except as a person in

117

a photograph — until now.'

Hannah laughed, gently.

'I'd best explain. Our father married twice, honey. My mother divorced him — oh, don't look so shocked, it's quite legal in some of the States — and later married your own mother. My brother died in the war between the States.' For a moment she was quiet, and sad. 'I kept in touch with Father, and he always saw to it that we were looked after while we were young.'

So that's where some of the money went, thought Amy, but said nothing.

'My mother remarried. A wealthy man, who'd made a lot of money out of the war. No class, honey, but money. I had gathered from his letters that our father thought he'd done enough for me. And there's something else.' She paused, and her shrewd dark eyes studied Amy's pale face briefly, as if she were trying to come to a decision. 'Well, never mind that for now. To continue. I had a letter from a man called Samuel McIntyre, telling me that our father had died in an accident, and that he'd left a rich gold-mine called the Royal Edward.'

'It wasn't an accident. Father had a weak heart and died when part of the mine collapsed. And it isn't a rich gold-mine — not yet. It isn't being worked, and, oh,

118

everything is rather complicated.'

'Are you telling me that I've come to this forsaken hole of a township for nothing?' Hannah's voice lost its velvet quality, and her American accent became much more marked, while the fingers of her left hand, ringed on the fore and middle fingers, but bare on the third, drummed on the arm of her chair. 'Honey, this needs some explaining. Can you accommodate us here? When I asked about rooms at one of the hotels, the manager told me that there was already a Miss Felstead here in town, living in the late Mr Felstead's house, which is how we came to be on the spot when you fainted.'

'Yes, there's room.'

'I'll send Polly out for our luggage. I daresay you can squeeze her in too?'

'Of course.'

But her half-sister's arrival at this time seemed too pat, too opportune. At great expense, Hannah had travelled from America in hope of sharing in the profits from a gold-mine. Hannah was not mentioned in their father's will, but, obviously, she was after her share.

Not the least puzzling aspect of this development was that she had been lured hither by the mysterious McIntyre.

Was Samuel McIntyre, after all, the person

behind those loathesome 'jokes'? He had hailed from Ballarat. Could he possibly be the 'gent' Jane had boasted about?

Yet, it was comforting to have extra people in the house, although Jane Kestle grumbled and made it clear that she had understood that she would have to 'do' for only one. Hannah generously tipped the man who brought round her luggage — a trunk and two valises, for the elder Miss Felstead did not travel light — and complained about the size of the main bedroom.

'The rooms at the hotel are smaller,' Amy pointed out, and Hannah, who, to be kind about it, was tired after a long journey, uttered a tinkling laugh.

'I'm sorry, honey. I keep forgetting that we're in the wilds of darkest Australia.'

Dr Jago called again after dinner, explaining that this was a quick, friendly visit to enquire whether Miss Amy had recovered from her indisposition.

'I fainted,' said Amy, firmly, 'because someone scared me.'

She then sketched in how she had found the spider, and what she had guessed was curiosity on his part, to see the other Miss Felstead again, changed to concern.

'Can you describe the spider?'

She told him as best she could, and

120

he dispensed the verdict that the small creature was of a harmless variety known to some as the tri-antelope, this strange word being a corruption of tarantula, which European spider it was said to resemble. More correctly, it was a huntsman, and although so fearsome in appearance, the bite was not venomous, and capturing and placing one in a box could be done with little risk.

'Ugh!' said Hannah.

'I know I'm foolish,' admitted Amy, appreciating that the doctor was trying to cheer her, 'but I can't abide spiders of any kind. Just to see one makes me feel quite ill.'

'Some people are like that about cats,' nodded Dr Jago, unconsciously repeating what Langdon Firebrace had said on the same subject. 'Does anyone know about this, Miss Felstead?'

She hesitated, remembering very well that climb up a narrow and awkward path when she had almost lost her balance, and Langdon Firebrace had reached out and taken her hand in his. How easy it would have been for him to let her drop to her death and explain it away as an accident.

'My relatives at home knew,' she said, dodging the question without telling an outright lie. Her reasons were a little mixed. She could not altogether trust Dr Jago, and there was always in her an unwillingness to accept that Langdon Firebrace was in fact her tormentor.

'It's the sort a thing a little boy'd do. You know how they are about frogs and so forth. It wouldn't be one of those little devils at the school, would it?'

Boys were in the minority at Mrs Stacey's school, which catered mostly for girls. However, there was a scattering of male pupils who were considered too young by their parents for the harsher life of boarding school. One or two of these, Amy knew, were blatantly mischievous, as a counter, she suspected, to petticoat government. She had not thought until now that one of these very young lads could have been the culprit.

'Perhaps,' she agreed, unconvinced.

'It's only a suggestion, but it might be wise to keep this latest episode to ourselves. If the same person is responsible, he may show his hand.'

When the doctor had left, Hannah came straight to the point.

'It's quite plain to me that I've landed in the middle of something. You'd best explain, honey.'

Once again, Amy hesitated, fighting uneasiness. Then she thought, if this stranger had any foreknowledge of what has been happening here, there can be no harm in telling her, So, she recounted the whole story, her hopeful voyage from England, the disappointing arrival, and the frightening practical jokes which seemed designed to make her leave.

'This man Firebrace. What is he like?'

'I don't know. He seems so — so pleasant. I can't make up my mind.'

'H'm.' Hannah seemed slightly amused. 'Is he good-looking?'

Amy made a pretence of poking at the fire.

'Yes,' she said, after a moment.

'Oh.'

The monosyllable carried a wealth of implication, overlaid with worldly amusement, and after this Hannah sat quietly for some moments, eyes narrowed in thought.

'I think I see,' she announced then, without explaining exactly what it was she did see, and smothered a yawn. 'Well, I'm for bed. I've never in my life been so jolted and battered as I was in that coach today.'

Another aspect of Hannah's arrival was revealed the next morning. Doing a little shopping in Firebrace's main street, Amy encountered Oscar Howarth of the *Gazette*.

'Life's full of surprises, eh?' he said, with forced jocularity, for he showed signs of the previous night's heavy drinking. 'I never guessed that Edmund had been married twice. Never said a word about it.'

Amy did not wish to discuss it, but the newspaper man was persistent.

'The other Miss Felstead had a shock when she found out that her little sister was already here! I was watching the passengers coming off the coach — always on the lookout for a bit of fresh news to liven up the old rag — and she was surprised, all right. Bit of a sensation, she was, especially with that black maid in tow.'

Mr Howarth was engaged in that spurious occupation known as setting a sprat to catch a mackerel. Miss Hannah's prosperous and elegant appearance had him agog, but Amy merely smiled.

'It was a great surprise to us both,' she admitted.

'Y'know, Miss Felstead, business people here in town are becoming anxious about the future. There's talk of a public meeting to discuss what's going to happen when the Western Consolidated runs down. Now that your sister is here, I expect you'll be coming

124

to some sort of decision about Edmund's mine.'

'I'm afraid I can't discuss anything, Mr Howarth. The matter is in the hands of my solicitor.'

Howarth did not look pleased, but he had something else to say.

'Read the *Gazette* on Monday, Miss Felstead. You'll learn what's going on round here.'

It was a relief to leave him and go into the post office to collect the mail which had arrived for her late the previous day. His every utterance had been disturbing, especially that concerning Hannah, who must have soon hidden her initial dismay on learning about Amy. Neither could Amy imagine what there would be to interest her in Monday's issue of the *Gazette*.

There were three letters awaiting her, one from Charlie Henthorne, one from Mr Parker, and another from the firm of Ballarat surveyors to whom she had written regarding Samuel McIntyre. The last she tore open as soon as she regained the street. The contents were a disappointment. Mr McIntyre had left their employ to work for Mr Felstead during the previous December, and they had no knowledge of his present whereabouts.

Reading Mr Parker's letter at home, she

could hear, at the rear of the house, a sharp exchange between Polly and Jane Kestle. The two servants had taken an instant dislike to each other.

'Perhaps I should agree,' she sighed, thinking aloud. 'Take the money and go back to England.'

Hannah sat alongside her with a rustle of the embellished grey silk which was so unsuitable for a Saturday morning at home.

'Why, honey, is it bad news?'

'Not really. Only it's all so complicated — and, well, I'm tired of the whole thing already.'

Mr Parker had informed her that the Firebraces' solicitors were willing to affect a compromise on behalf of their clients. The Firebrace family was ready to admit their late brother's indebtedness to the late Mr Edmund Felstead, and would make a cash settlement for the exact amount involved on condition that the real estate handed over to the late Mr Felstead was returned to the family.

After a moment's hesitation, Amy handed this missive to Hannah for her inspection, and glanced through Charlie's letter. He was missing her so much, and was still hopeful that she would change her mind, as he worried constantly about the effects of wild Australian conditions on her health. Elspeth had told him that she felt sure that Amy would soon tire of the colonies and return Home to her family and the friends who cared so much for her.

I detest people who try to make up my mind for me, thought Amy, and tucked the refolded letter into her pocket.

'Well,' said Hannah, after reading through Mr Parker's letter twice, 'these Firebrace people surely are most determined to get their hands on that mine again. I expect that now they've scared the wits out of you, they think you'll give in. Not that it means much to me!'

As Hannah uttered those words, she laughed, curtly, and without humour.

'I'm sorry that you've had such a long journey for very little, but you can hardly blame me!' retorted Amy, now on the defensive. 'I didn't even know of your existence until yesterday.'

'Oh, honey, I'm sorry. I know it isn't your fault!' The other smiled winningly. 'But the letter I had from that man McIntyre was so full of promises.'

Amy decided to show her half-sister the letter she had received in the post that day, and Hannah's mouth set thinly as she read it through.

'I intend to get to the bottom of this,' she declared, 'even if I gain nothing. Just for the satisfaction, you might say. When I catch up with Mr McIntyre, he'll have some explaining to do, you can rest on that!'

11

Any plans which Hannah may have had for commencing her investigations into McIntyre's disappearance had to be postponed, for at about lunch-time it began to rain, and continued to rain throughout the afternoon, the night, and Sunday.

Amy, tired of the bickering between the servants, allowed Jane Kestle to visit her uncle during the afternoon, and watching the young girl scurrying off, head low under an umbrella, Hannah grimaced.

'A common little snip,' was her verdict. 'Was she all you could find out here?'

'I'm afraid I allowed myself to be talked into hiring her by her aunt, who kept the house clean while it was empty. I feel sorry for her, in a way. If she lost this place, I doubt whether she could find another in Firebrace.'

'You shouldn't let your heart rule your head.' Hannah was plainly bored and seeking about for some way of occupying herself. 'Amy, was there anything missing from Father's desk?'

'No, I don't think so.'

129

'Strange. Let's have another look.'

Half an hour of sorting and checking revealed nothing of further interest, until Hannah, with a rather exaggerated gesture, clasped one long-fingered, beringed hand to her smooth forehead.

'Of course! A secret drawer! My stepfather's desk had a secret drawer where he kept some gold, in case of emergencies, he always said.'

The past tense interested Amy.

'Is your stepfather still alive?' she asked, politely.

'Oh, yes. I haven't lived at home for a long time.'

'Are you married, Hannah?'

'Married?' Hannah laughed. 'No, I value my freedom, honey.'

As she spoke, she felt deftly about the desk, with no immediate result.

Amy dropped to her knees, and made a few measurements with her fingers.

'Look,' she said, 'how deep it is under here.'

'Ah!' exclaimed Hannah, bending, and prodding, until a flange, so perfectly fitted that there was no betraying crack in the surface, fell forward, revealing a cavity behind.

'I was right,' declared the American

gleefully, but soon her expression changed. There were no papers in the compartment, only a revolver and a flat box containing ammunition.

Hannah took out both objects.

'It's new,' she said. 'A very recent design, I'd say. Loaded, too.' She removed the bullets with an expertise which startled Amy, to whom firearms were a mystery. 'I don't like loaded guns,' she continued. 'Now, I wonder why our father kept this in his desk.'

'Robbers? Or perhaps he'd had to endure what I have been experiencing.'

'Habit, most likely,' said Hannah, putting the revolver and box back into the hiding place. 'He'd led a roving life.'

Amy lay awake for a long time that night. The rain pounding down on the iron roof was ceaseless, and in the distance she could hear a steady roar, identified the next day as Fish Creek, swirling over its banks as it carried its burden of clay-stained water into the swamp system which in turn gave birth to another, larger river. She did not go to church, but filled in the morning writing letters to Elspeth and, after thought, to Charlie. His declaration of continuing devotion had touched her: it was the one steady thing in an uneasy world. She did not wish to marry him, but neither did she wish to lose his friendship.

Hannah stayed in bed until eleven. Then, aided by Polly, she devoted a full hour to her toilette. Mac, allowed indoors by Amy who had taken pity on his wet and woebegone state, greeted Hannah feverishly as the elder sister swished out to a simple lunch in considerable grandeur. Amy recollected that dogs were said to be infallible judges of good character. She tried to accept this to settle her disquiet about Hannah.

During the school lunch break the following day, she slipped out and bought the latest copy of the *Gazette*. The front page, as usual, was devoted to advertisements ranging from the information that Bolitho's Drapery now stocked the latest in ladies' summer apparel to a somewhat bald statement regarding the capabilities of a stallion. The leading news story inside concerned what must have been an extremely long and tedious meeting by members of the local road board, followed by intelligence of a prize won by a local vigneron at the Adelaide Agricultural Show. Stock market reports, fill-in pieces clipped from overseas papers about such diverse topics as the prevalence of icebergs in the North Atlantic and more plotting in the Balkans, a local wedding . . . Amy was ready to give up in disgust when, like so many readers who tend to leave the most taxing item to the last, she returned to the editorial.

The heading was innocuous: 'OUR TOWN'. Underneath, Mr Oscar Howarth flung out a challenge.

'We all like our town. We like its location betwixt Dividing Ranges and Grampians. We like the spirit of British endeavour which has built it from a collection of tents and shanties into the thriving sub-metropolis of today. We like it because it is a good town, free of the back-slums and moral defects of large cities.

'We like to think that in our town there flourishes that splendid spirit of independence, of every man being the equal of his fellows, which is guiding our great southern continent to its Manifest Destiny.

'Why then, do we denigrate our town with an unfitting name, a name which fell upon it by chance, the name of the owner of the sheep run, long gone, which once spread where our houses stand today?

'We need a new name! A fitting name! A name which expresses rightfully the mainspring of our town!

'This newspaper hereby initiates a competition, open to all, to produce a name worthy of us. Ten pounds will be awarded to the person who submits the name considered most suitable by a panel of judges, and representation will be made to Parliament so that a permanent change may be effected.'

So this was Mr Howarth's bombshell. To Amy, essentially an outsider, it was a damp squib, but the editor had touched off a controversy which would divide the town into two classes for years to come.

The same afternoon, Langdon Firebrace was waiting for Amy outside the school, seated in his buggy, with little Avis Jago at his side. That betraying thump of the heart started as soon as she saw him, but nonetheless, Amy resolutely intended to walk past with no more than a nod.

'I'll take you home,' he called out, and sprung down to assist her on to the seat.

'I prefer to walk,' she said, in a low voice, and promptly stepped into one of the large puddles left by the weekend's rain.

'You'd be much safer riding,' he rejoindered, and before she could protest, she had been handed up and was sitting alongside the child.

'Avis's governess is in bed with a cold today,' he explained, climbing up himself and taking the reins in his strong hands. Then, casually, 'I suppose you were a governess before you emigrated?'

'No. I was not. I lived with my uncle — actually my mother's uncle — and his daughter.'

'Ah, an unpaid secretary and general dogsbody. What is politely called a companion, no doubt.'

It was so accurate that she felt like hitting him.

'I was very happy with my lot.'

'Then why did you make such haste to come out here? All this wrangle over the mine could have been conducted without your presence here.'

'That would have pleased you, no doubt.'

'Miss Felstead, must you snap at me every time I try to make a friendly approach?'

She had been so engrossed in thinking out crushing responses that she had not noticed that instead of progressing towards her home, they were going in the opposite direction.

'Mr Firebrace! Where are you taking me?' Visions of being kidnapped snapped into her mind, and she was poised to leap for freedom, at risk to bone and flesh.

'I'm taking you home. The long way about. It's time you saw something of the place. In any case, I'd promised to deliver Avis to her father for the night, but he won't be home until five. Now, look across there!'

They were on a low rise a few hundred yards along the westerly road leading out of Firebrace. He had reined in the horses, and through a break in the trees she could see waters gleaming in the late afternoon sunshine.

'That's the Great Swamp. It's full to the brim after the rain we've had this spring, and the frogs are beside themselves with joy.'

It was little wonder that Avis put her hands to her ears in mock distress.

Big frogs, little frogs, bass frogs and soprano frogs all combined to grind out a deafening barrage of sound which could have been beautiful only to other frogs.

'When I was a boy,' went on the man, 'the blacks used to come from all over this part of Victoria to the Great Swamp to feast on eels. There were only a few dozen people in the local tribe, but they'd be here in their hundreds, talking several different languages, but keeping the peace amongst themselves. It was an arrangement going back thousands of years, they told my father, and in those days you could see the channels they'd dug to make catching the eels easier for themselves.'

He turned the buggy back towards the town, and Amy spoke after a short silence.

'I dare say you're very annoyed about Mr

136

Howarth's attempt to find a more suitable name for this town,' she announced, and he laughed.

'Why should I be? I find sharing my name with the town an embarrassment. Though if Howarth had dug more deeply, he'd have known that we never referred to our original run as the Firebrace run. It was always called Eoke, the blacks' name for the place. Very appropriate, too. The word means eel.'

That, thought Amy, is the most aggravating thing about this man. One would have expected him to be angry, but he took a completely rational view.

'In fact,' he continued, 'I think I shall submit the name myself. Can you imagine old Howarth's face when he opens an entry from me?'

Amy could. There was nothing worse than trying to fight someone who was determined to be agreeable.

It was a relief, she told herself, to part company from him at her gate, but having set down little Avis outside the doctor's house and told her to run inside and give her father a surprise, he quickly caught up with Amy. Hannah Felstead, with adoring Mac at her hem, sauntered out at the same time, her face brightening at the sight of a personable man.

137

There was nothing for it but to introduce them, and Mr Firebrace was immediately all charm. Then he stated what had caused him to seek out Amy that day.

'I do hope that you're both free next Sunday afternoon,' he said, producing a sealed envelope from an inner pocket. 'It's our custom to hold a garden party each spring when shearing's over. Weather permitting, we hope to have luncheon in the open air, and croquet and other light entertainment during the afternoon. Our garden is only ten years old, and can't match those of older countries, but it's considered the best hereabouts.'

'How absolutely delightful!' gushed Hannah before the young woman could utter a sound. 'Of course we shall come. How very kind of you to invite us!' She took the envelope from his outstretched fingers. 'Our invitation? But how shall we send our reply? Is mail delivered to your home?'

'Give it to Dr Jago. And I'll ask him to bring you out.' As he spoke, he was looking at the dog with some puzzlement. 'That beast's made himself at home. I thought Eric had taken him. Heaven only knows why. He's the most useless dog I've ever come up against.'

Still, he smiled at Mac, and leaned down

138

to rub the dog behind the ears before departing.

'So, that's our villain,' said Hannah slowly, relishing every word, as Mr Firebrace drove away. 'Honey, what does one wear to a garden party in the Australian bush?'

Amy scarcely heard her. She was trying to understand exactly why Dr Jago had provided her with Mac, declared by Mr Firebrace to be completely useless. She had already suspected this: Mac had an unlimited propensity for making friends.

'I've had a busy day,' Hannah remarked, as they went indoors. 'It's just as well I did come. You've needed someone here with a bit more push. Now, listen.'

Amy sat down wearily, whilst Hannah, careful of her elaborately draped black skirts, perched on another chair.

'I did a little shopping today, and asked here and there about this man McIntyre. No one thought much of him. He left debts everywhere when he skipped town. I dare say he hoped to part me from some money. But that's not all. I've arranged for a proper headstone over our father's grave, honey.'

They had already discussed this. Hannah set great store by impressive graveyard monuments, it seemed, and had brushed aside Amy's explanation for tardiness in this matter being due to the delays in settling the estate.

'As I was leaving the stonemason's, I noticed a little building opposite with the notice 'Goldfields' Warden'. So over I went, and introduced myself. A charming man! I learnt two things. One, that your friend Mr Firebrace has requested him to declare the Royal Edward out of bounds to all parties until things are resolved.'

'Oh,' said Amy. 'Oh!'

She forgot the wearisome details of this long day and sat bolt upright. Langdon Firebrace, who not an hour since had been so very pleasant, even to inviting the Misses Felstead to a socially desirable function at his home, was once again concealing his true purpose behind a smiling mask.

'And, my dear, that isn't all. Oh, no, not by a long chalk.' Hannah's handsome face was smugly triumphant. 'Mr Haines — the warden — inspected the mine after our father died. He also gave evidence at the inquest. One of the witnesses was a blackfellow called Jimmy, who is, I understand, a sort of protégé of Mr Firebrace's. At least, Mr Firebrace sees to it that this Jimmy and his nephew always have something to eat. But this Jimmy happened to be near the mine when the accident happened, and he said that he heard a crack, almost like a gunshot, and then Mr McIntyre came running out calling for help.'

'But our father died of heart failure. Dr Jago told me so.'

'One moment. When Mr McIntyre was questioned, he said that he heard the cracking sound also, but thought it was caused by the movement of rock.'

Amy frowned as she thought this over.

'Exactly what do you mean, Hannah?'

'I mean that perhaps someone knew about our father's bad heart. A shot fired inside the mine wouldn't sound very loud outside, but it would reverberate inside, and could be enough to kill someone with shock if that person had a weak heart.'

'You mean that Mr McIntyre did that?'

'Perhaps, and perhaps not. There could have been another person in the mine. I dare say the Royal Edward is like other mines — there isn't only one tunnel, but little side passages and shafts going in all directions.'

'But wouldn't the blackfellow have seen another person going in?' Then Hannah's exact meaning began to sink in. During the confusion after the tragedy, a third party could have slipped away, and even Jimmy's sharp and observant aboriginal eyes would

141

have 'missed' one particular person.

'And I'm willing to wager that the last thing Mr Firebrace ever expected was that you'd actually come to Australia, or myself, as far as that goes.'

'If only we could find this Mr McIntyre and ask him. He could explain so much!'

Hannah smiled, conspiratorially.

'It's up to you, honey, to worm what you can out of our Mr Firebrace next Sunday. He might want that mine, but he's also attracted to you, so go out of your way to charm him!'

12

If Mr Firebrace had waited for a thousand years and sifted through every October day during that time, he could not have chosen one more suitable for the garden party. It was the sort of day which comes rarely in southern Australia, when the sun warms without baking, a breeze tempers without turning into a gale, and an occasional fluffy white cloud scuds across the vast blue sky to provide ornamentation rather than threat of inclemency.

Miss Firebrace welcomed Amy and Hannah without any real warmth, but little Avis Jago slipped through the women's skirts to take Amy's hand.

'Is Mac being a good dog?' she asked.

'Of course he is.' She glanced about and saw Dr Jago approaching from the direction of the stables. 'Come along and talk to your father.'

It was a good way of escaping from Miss Firebrace's unfriendly manner. Hannah, impressive in mulberry silk, was, as usual, full of undaunted self-confidence, not shared by her half-sister.

Typically, Hannah had instructed Amy what to do and say when she found herself alone with Mr Firebrace. She must *not* mention that they knew that he had approached the warden about placing the mine out of bounds. This would put him on his guard. But she must ask, oh, so innocently, about Mr McIntyre and carefully watch for a reaction, a twitch of the mouth, a tensing of the hands, a stiffening of the neck sinews. The most composed people could not entirely hide their reactions, said Hannah. But Amy must not look into his eyes, hoping to see guilt there. Mr Firebrace was obviously an accomplished flirt, and he would simply distract her.

Avis went off with her father, and a voice spoke in Amy's ear, sending her senses reeling and making her cling determinedly to Hannah's advice.

'Hullo! Sorry I didn't notice you arrive. You look absolutely stunning!' Her host was at her side. 'And your sister! You'll both set the whole district on its heels.'

There was only one thing to do when the conversation took such blatantly personal lines, and that was to steer it into safer, duller courses.

'Your gardens are very well laid out, Mr Firebrace. I hadn't realised on my earlier visit just how extensive they are.'

'I'll show you round, later. But first, Miss Felstead, could I interest you in a glass of champagne?'

He was very much the courteous host, steering her into a group of young people, some of whom had travelled many miles to be here today, and making introductions. Hannah had already found a group of her own, although it was noticeable that it was mostly male and that looks she was receiving from other women were thoughtful rather than admiring.

Lunch, laid out on white-clothed trestles, could not be faulted, but not everyone was in a mood of uncritical pleasure. By chance, Amy found herself standing next to Dr Jago and Miss Firebrace, and with an earnest young man claiming her attention, she could not walk away and thus avoid overhearing a low-spoken conversation.

'Well, Allison, I notice Avis isn't as shy as she was. I'm glad to see her playing so easily with the other children. She'll fit into school without any trouble, I'm sure.'

'There's no reason why she shouldn't stay here, with a governess, Eric. Actually, I think that Miss McDougall is quite superior to Mrs Stacey, or her school. And I'm quite capable of teaching Avis music, as well you know.

She's used to us here.'

'I'm her father, Allison. It's time she came to me.'

Amy, trying hard to concentrate on her companion's description of a bivouac held by the local unit of volunteer rifles, caught a glimpse of Miss Firebrace's expression and felt a quiver of shock. Pure malevolence was in her eyes as she replied to the doctor's statement.

'Your life is so upset, Eric. Out all night, at everyone's beck and call. The child would be constantly in the care of your servants. She would be far better off with us.'

Amy put aside her plate, and took another glass of champagne to hide the fact that she was eavesdropping. Far from eating out her heart over her rejection years ago, Allison Firebrace, it seemed, was engaged in a long-drawn-out campaign of vengeance.

'Did you by any chance come across this naturalist fellow while you were out training?' It was Langdon Firebrace, putting the question to Amy's companion.

'Naturalist?'

'There's been talk of someone gathering specimens for a member of the Royal Family. I've wanted to meet him and show him what I'm doing here.'

'Lang's a bit of a fanatic, Miss Felstead,'

said the other man, with a laugh. 'He actually tries to grow native plants. We spend years clearing the bush from our land and sowing crops and pasture, but he's determined to undermine our hard work.'

'He has the wrong end of the stick. Don't listen to him, Miss Felstead. I've been experimenting this last year or so to adapt native plants to garden conditions.'

Not altogether unwillingly, she was led to a distant corner of the garden, where it was protected from harsh winds, partly by an angle of the homestead and partly by a brush fence. On the way, he took two glasses from a tray carried by Mary Anne Kestle, very trim in black and white, and handed one to Amy.

Heavens! Is he about to try to seduce me amidst the wheelbarrows and compost heaps, she thought, and suppressed a giggle.

'Some seeds of our natives are extremely hard to germinate,' he said, sipping champagne and changing from a black-dyed villain into a young man intent on sharing his enthusiasm. He pointed to the shallow boxes laid out under a glass roof. 'We dread fire in summer, but it's part of the life cycle of many Australian plants. Without being subjected to extreme heat, the pods can't open to release their seed.'

'You missed your vocation,' said Amy, trying to sound sharp and matter of fact, whilst being only too aware of his hand against her right elbow. 'You should have been a botanist.'

He laughed, ruefully.

'I had my heart set on science. Eighteen months at a German university weren't altogether wasted, however. My brother wasn't the type of heir my father had in mind, so I was recalled. Still, I've been able to apply some of my learning to the art of improving pastures — and putting life back into soil ruined by constant cropping. That was the tragedy of some of the miners who took up land herabouts, Amy. They knew next to nothing about farming, and, in any case, they had to plant crops year after year on the same ground because they couldn't afford to leave it fallow. Now it's up to those who've followed to repair the damage.'

This sounded different, somehow, to the tale told by Oscar Howarth, in which Langdon Firebrace had been a greedy scoundrel intent on grabbing land from the poor.

'Do you know,' she said, carefully, hoping to catch him off guard, 'anything about insects?'

'Only that most of them are a nuisance,'

148

he responded, after a moment. 'Oh, I was forgetting. You're the young lady who's so afraid of spiders.'

'Forgetting? Someone knew that I was afraid of spiders, Mr Firebrace, and it could only have been you.'

Later, looking back, she knew that it was the unaccustomed champagne which had loosened her tongue thus. Also, she knew that she had disobeyed Hannah's carefully thought-out ploy. She should have asked about McIntyre, thus giving away nothing and at the same time learning something. Instead, she blundered straight in with an accusation.

'What on earth are you talking about?'

'Someone has been trying to scare me, Mr Firebrace. You must have heard about it. The last attempt was with a spider. You're the only person in this part of the world — except those who heard after the event — who knew that I'm absolutely terrified of spiders.'

A long moment dragged past. She was conscious of the voices and laughter in the background, of horses neighing in the near distance, and of a sudden cackle from a hen in the poultry yard.

'Well,' he said. 'That's a splendid state of affairs! I'm doing my best to be pleasant, and you're telling me I'm responsible for playing a half-witted practical joke.'

'Jokes, Mr Firebrace.'

'Look, you've the town's trollop for a maid, and you wonder . . . Hadn't it occurred to you that these jokes were directed against Jane?'

'Yes. And I don't believe it.' Belatedly, she remembered Hannah's instructions, and again belied them. 'As well, Mr Firebrace, now everything is out in the open, I'm quite aware that you've gone behind my back and had my mine placed legally out of bounds.'

The bemusement on his face was replaced by anger.

'All right, Miss Felstead. I asked the warden to step in. It should have been arranged right from the start, and there should be a letter in the post for you about it. Some idiot has been entering the mine. Whether it was you, or someone in your pay, I've no means of knowing, but that mine is dangerous, and I won't have it.'

'Were you frightened that someone might take samples and find out that your story of the mine being worthless is a falsehood?'

He went pink, and then white, very white, the pallor of rage. Fortunately, at that moment, someone called his name.

'I'll deal with you later,' he whispered at

Amy, and strode away.

She leaned against a post, dizzy, and wanting, foolishly, to cry.

Miss Firebrace was to entertain the guests to a brief recital. She was a gifted pianist, with quite a reputation musically amongst her circle of friends and acquaintances. Not everyone could crowd comfortably into the drawing-room, and so the overflow stood under the veranda outside the open french doors.

'Did you find out anything?' demanded Hannah, rather crushed against Amy.

'Nothing.' Amy looked straight ahead, so that Hannah would not see that the mere mention of the subject started tears in her eyes.

'I found out something. His private study is two doors along the passage outside that door.'

'So?'

'He's out on the veranda. If you slip out no one will think anything of it. Ladies do have to leave the room, honey.'

'No.'

Hannah said no more, but Amy, trying to listen to Allison Firebrace's expert handling of a sonata, decided, gambler-like, to make this her last throw. Her father had taken chances a-plenty in his lifetime. As his daughter, it was required of her.

So, after a minute or so, she arose, and rustled past the other ladies with a demure 'Excuse me'. Out in the passage, she took a deep breath, and tried two doors before she found the correct one. Guiltily, she slipped into the study and shut the door behind her. Now what?

Amy had no very clear idea for what she was looking, and as she stood there, uncertain, the truth hit her with great force. Even if incriminating evidence had been stacked in plain view, she would not have wished to find it.

As if to compound this discovery, there was a sound at the window, one of the doors was pushed open, and Langdon Firebrace stepped into the room, pulling the curtains together behind him.

'Now,' he said, a brittle edge to his voice, 'what do you hope to find in here? My signed confession to all sorts of villainy?'

'I missed my way,' she replied, stiffly, trying to maintain her dignity and wishing that he was not so handsome.

'You didn't miss your way. You came in here to pry.' As he spoke, he locked the door and pocketed the key.

'Unlock that door this instant!'

He shook his head, and she turned to leave

through the french window.

'Do that,' he threatened, 'and I'll cry out 'Stop, thief!' '

'You're behaving quite dreadfully, not at all as a gentleman should.' Her voice was haughty, but her knees were trembling.

'Of course. You're sure that I'm a scoundrel, so I'm going to act like a scoundrel to please you.'

'Stop!' she protested. 'What on earth are you doing?'

'I'm taking off your hat so that I can kiss you without pulling your hair away.'

And he placed her Dolly Varden hat, with its pins alongside, on the desk.

'Let me go!' she said, a moment later, not very strongly.

She knew, of course, that she should have screamed, stamped on his feet, or otherwise behaved in a way of which Cousin Elspeth would have approved. Instead, when he kissed her, very hard, on the mouth, she sighed, and her arms, acting of their own volition, slid up about his neck. Vaguely, a minute or so having passed, she became aware that they were on the sofa, half-reclining in a most abandoned fashion.

'Isn't that better,' said Langdon Firebrace, 'than trying to start a quarrel every time we meet?'

'I find your behaviour reprehensible,' she answered, sitting up straight, and musing, with some wonder, that she had ever thought Charlie Henthorne good at kissing.

'No worse than yours, sneaking into my study for heaven only knows what reason.'

He placed a gentle finger beneath her chin, tipped up her face, and kissed her again, lightly.

'I must go,' he whispered. 'I came in, you know, to find a cigar-cutter. I didn't expect to be so charmingly distracted.'

Sanity struggled to the surface. So far, she had made a thorough mess of trying to carry out Hannah's plans, but one thing she would do.

'Mr Firebrace,' she said, rather incongruously, considering that her face was pressed against his shoulder, 'what became of Mr McIntyre?'

Now he was the one to sit up straight.

'What a time to talk about that good-for-nothing fellow,' he responded, and raised himself to his feet, looking down at her quizzically. 'Now, my blue-eyed angel, why do you want to know about McIntyre at this very instant?'

'Because he's missing.'

'Who told you that?' He turned away as he spoke, and rummaged through a drawer

in the desk, ostensibly to find the cigar-
cutter, or was it to hide the expression on
his face?

'No one knows what became of him.'

'I dare say that pleases him. He owned
money all over the town. Ha, here it is.'

As he held up the missing cigar-cutter,
someone outside called his name, and he
took the key from his pocket and handed
it to Amy.

'There you are, Miss Felstead. We'll
discuss McIntyre when next we meet.'

A touch on the cheek with his forefinger,
and she was alone.

'You're very quiet,' said Hannah, when
they had reached home, for they had
been forced to keep conversation in careful
channels in Dr Jago's company.

'The wine and the sun were rather much.
This is the first warm day we've had since I
arrived. I've a splitting headache.'

'I must admit that I expected something
dull and rural, but the food was quite
splendid — and all those handsome men!
Mind you, they talk of nothing but sheep
and horses — and with broad Scots accents
in most cases! Now, tell me, what happened
in the study?'

'Nothing, really.' Amy sounded so innocent
that it was patently false.

'Oh, honey! You can confide in me! I know that one must exert oneself a little at times to twist a man the way one wants.'

How unbearably cheap Hannah made it sound. And it hadn't been like that at all. For Amy, being in Langdon Firebrace's arms had been the most wonderful experience of her life.

'I asked Mr Firebrace about McIntyre. He came in and caught me in the study, you know. I was very embarrassed and said that I'd missed my way.'

'Ah!' said Hannah, and cocked her head on one side. 'To be honest, Amy, I didn't think you had the sense to turn such a situation to your advantage. What did he say about McIntyre?'

'Only that McIntyre owed money right and left,' replied Amy, nettled, but determined to retain her poise. 'Mr Firebrace says that is why he left in such a hurry.'

Hannah was visibly disappointed.

'We knew that already. Still, the day wasn't altogether wasted. I discussed those wretched practical jokes with Dr Jago. He blames one of Jane Kestle's admirers, but I think I know the reason for them.'

Amy forgot her headache and her annoyance at Hannah's prying.

'You do?'

156

'Yes. A poltergeist.'

Amy could hardly credit that she had heard Hannah say such a thing. Poltergeist indeed! Things which went bump in the night, and made subject matter for spooky stories told about a fire on dark and stormy nights were poltergeists. In cold daylight, they were only loose shutters and sinking foundations.

'You cannot be serious,' she gasped.

'Never more serious, honey. Poltergeists are real enough, believe me. I could tell you . . . Never mind. Of course, I wouldn't put much past Miss Firebrace. There's a sour creature for you. She likes her life as it is, living in her brother's house and ruling the roost, and raising a child in her own pattern. She sees you as a threat. I noticed her expression when she was watching you, and if looks could have killed, honey, you'd be stone dead.'

As Amy watched her half-sister's bustled back swaying gracefully towards her own bedroom to be helped out of her elaborate costume by the faithful Polly, she was thoughtful. Hannah had displayed a new and disturbing facet of her character today at the garden party. She was able to consume an astonishing amount of champagne without disgracing herself.

Still, Hannah's comments had opened up

157

a fresh field of thought. What experiences lay in her kinswoman's past which made her believe in poltergeists? She guessed, too, that Hannah's comments about Miss Allison Firebrace were at least partly correct. Miss Allison showed every sign of being a vindictive woman who kept her grudges alive for a long time.

But . . . Would a poltergeist or Miss Allison poison a dog? A silly, harmless dog which had failed as a sheepdog and was quite unsuited to the job of watchdog?

A passing workman saw the poor stiff body on the grass early the following morning, and moved the corpse out of sight so that the ladies would not be upset. Amy cried when she was told, and Hannah, dressed to the nines, went to the police.

13

The policeman took a serious view of the incident, and so did his sergeant. Baits in town, where they could be found by little children, were extremely dangerous, and the kind of person who poisoned domestic dogs was a shingle short.

He questioned Jane Kestle at length. It was common knowledge that young Jack Beaton still hankered after Jane, although why he wasted his time on her when there were plenty of decent girls waiting to be courted — even if he did want to fight the world when he'd had a few drinks — baffled Constable Price. And Jack was fond of dogs.

Constable Price was of the opinion that Miss Amy Felstead had brought trouble with her, and as for the other, with all those flashing rings and none on the correct finger, well, he wasn't one to say anything without proof.

Yes, Firebrace had been a better place without the Felstead sisters, or half-sisters, as they really were. Old Felstead, with his talk of opening up the Royal Edward and his slanging matches with Mr Firebrace, had been nowhere near such a nuisance as pretty Miss Amy and the odd things which had happened at her house. That's what came, he thought, of young women traipsing about the globe on their own and setting up house without a husband or sensible male relative to keep a hold on things.

Jane Kestle resisted his questions with a sulky stubbornness which made Constable Price threaten talking to her parents about her.

'Good chapel folk, they are,' he said, 'which is more than can be said for you, Miss. Where've you been these last Sundays, eh?'

Jane's full mouth pouted.

'I've been too busy, looking after this house, an' th' dinner to get, an' all.'

During that same evening, Jane disappeared, taking with her a bundle of clothing, the money from Hannah's purse, and Amy's Dolly Varden hat.

'Off to this man she was talking about,' commented Hannah dryly, the next morning, when Polly reported the unfired stove and empty bed. 'Have you any idea of whom this admirer of hers might be? I don't mind the silly slut eloping, but I do mind having my money stolen.'

'Only that he was better than Jack Beaton. Jack is a young man who works for Mr Firebrace.' Amy wearily pushed a strand of hair up from her eyes. 'She claimed that he was a gentleman.'

'To that trash, anyone who changes his socks twice a week is a gentleman,' snorted Polly in the background.

'I'm going to report her to the police. She's a thief,' seethed Hannah, who was still in her dressing-gown.

'No, don't bother. I'm sick of all this fuss,' said Amy, thrusting a pin through her everyday hat to keep it in place. Glancing at her reflection in the mirror of the hallstand, she could see the pallor brought about by two restless nights, when sleep was only fitful between times when thoughts churned endlessly.

On the way to the school, she collected her mail. There was only one letter, from Elspeth. Her father, Amy's great-uncle, was not very well and feeling his years. Life had been very quiet in the village. Their little run of local excitement, the burglaries and so on, had ended before Amy had left, and although one had to be thankful that there had been no more crime and tragedy, there were none but trivialities to report.

As she went in to face her class, a longing

for the dull peace she had left behind seized the girl. The strain of the past weeks was now dimming the growing intolerance she had felt towards life in Uncle Theo's house. Whoever it was who had played those cruel tricks had cause to feel satisfied with his — or her — self. Amy Felstead was fast reaching the end of her tether.

Pausing to watch a huge flock of white and yellow cockatoos as she walked homewards on that mild afternoon, she made up her mind. Tonight, she would write to Mr Parker and instruct him to accept the opposition's offer of a cash settlement in exchange for the disputed real estate. No longer could she stand being torn apart by suspicions made all the more unbearable because she had fallen in love with Langdon Firebrace. How Hannah would react to this decision, she could not anticipate, and neither did she really care.

Stronger, and more dominant, was the memory of the occasion when she had wondered whether Langdon Firebrace was the man to whom Jane Kestle had referred. Amy remembered his lips so hard and demanding on her own, his arms holding her so firmly and yet so gently, and distaste washed through her.

She entered the house, pulling off her hat

in a weary movement.

He stood framed in the door to the parlour, wearing his day-to-day uniform of well-worn riding clothes, smiling at her in a way which sent her senses, always so traitorous, into a mixture of hope and shyness.

'Hullo, Amy,' he said.

'What are you doing here?' She was on the defensive.

'Paying a call. I thought you'd never come.'

'Is my sister home?' It suddenly became important that they should not be alone.

'She is, her maid told me, out on an errand. I want to talk to you.'

She allowed herself to be ushered into the parlour, conscious of the illogical desires filling her whole being. He waited until she had seated herself, primly, on a cedar chair, and then perched astride another similar chair, resting his arms on the back, and regarding her seriously.

'Why do you wish to talk with me?' She tried hard to sound distant and dignified, but her voice faltered.

'Why shouldn't I wish to talk to you, Amy? I rather gathered that we were — um — courting. Now, first of all, what's all this about poor Mac? Eric told me this morning when he came out to look at one of the men.

Amy, I hadn't realised that there'd been so many of these incidents. You poor girl!'

'I thought that Dr Jago would have kept you well informed.'

'Why? Eric and I aren't that close. Poor old Mac! The stupidest dog I've ever known. Useless as a working dog. The sort of dog that'd make friends with a bushranger when he was holding up the homestead.'

'Then why was he offered as a watchdog by your sister?' She shot the question at him, suddenly not trusting him at all. Why did he have to be so easy in his manner, so sure that she accepted him as a suitor, and so much the master of the situation?

'My sister wouldn't do anything to oblige Eric Jago. If she thought he wanted a watchdog, she'd see to it that the one she offered was to the contrary.' He frowned, and shook his head, as if chasing away something unpleasant, and then reached out a hand so her. 'Come and sit on the sofa.'

She wanted to refuse, but again his touch filled her with that betraying desire, overwhelming her in a tide of un-reason and love.

'That's better,' he commented, as they reseated themselves, and he slipped an arm about her shoulders. 'Now, have you any idea at all who poisoned Mac? I can tell you, if I catch him, I'll tear him from limb to limb.'

'No, but Hannah said on Sunday that she thought a poltergeist was responsible for all the tricks. I'm afraid that I simply don't know what to think.' Even as she spoke, she wished that she had not mentioned Hannah's peculiar theory.

'A poltergeist? I didn't think that Miss Felstead was the type to believe such rubbish. Do you know exactly what is meant by a poltergeist?'

'An evil spirit, isn't it? I know there's a fad for spiritualism, but we never discussed it at home. Cousin Elspeth considered it all very wicked.'

'Poltergeist, my sweet, is German, and when Germans need a new word, they combine two or three which they already have. So, poltergeist is what it says, a noisy ghost. I've never met one personally, but I gathered that they threw things about the house, and broke china and so forth. A nuisance rather than dangerous. I wonder,' he continued, very slowly and thoughtfully, 'why Miss Hannah said such a thing?'

'I think she'd had rather a lot of champagne.'

'H'm. We'll forget it for the time being. There's something I must discuss with you,

165

and you must listen to me. It's about that damned mine. I've drafted out a letter to my solicitors telling them that I want them to hold their horses for a while, and what you must do, my dearest, is write a similar letter to your own fellow.' He spoke very quietly, and caressed her shoulder persuasively, rather like a man stroking a nervous cat.

'Oh!' She jerked away, angry and hurt that he should use her in this way. 'I'm not so easily swayed, Mr Firebrace.'

'For heaven's sake, girl, stop calling me Mr Firebrace. My name's Lang. Now, Amy, how in the world can we be involved in litigation if we're married?'

Those unbelievable words hung between them. How curious, she would think later, that she had not even considered marriage with Langdon Firebrace as a probability. She had seen their relationship in terms of a heavy flirtation, of herself acting foolishly, and with this dashing young man taking advantage of her weakness.

'I hardly know you.' Very true.

'I'm twenty-eight, going on twenty-nine,' he replied, with disarming good humour. 'I'm single, healthy, reasonably rich so long as the seasons are kind and wool prices keep up, and passably well educated. There are no convicts, or lunatics, as far as I know, in the family, and my father fell in love with my mother at first sight, which I never really believed until a few weeks ago.'

She remained silent, quite unable to speak.

'I'm not going down on my knees in front of you, like a comic character in *Punch*,' he murmured, kissing her tenderly. 'Think about it, darling Amy. I'm willing to wait all of two days for your answer. Then I'll come and shake it out of you.'

She laughed, and flung her arms about him.

'Of course I'll marry you, Lang!'

What of her inheritance, of the cruel 'jokes' which had made her life so wretched, of her resolve to return to the safety of Uncle Theo's home, and of the separated lady in Ballarat? They were still there, small grey shadows in the background, but dazzled out of sight by the blinding sunshine of the moment.

They held hands without speaking for a little while, until their enchantment was crudely shattered by the scream of the steam whistle over at the Western Consolidated Mine.

Amy had soon become used to the blast of the steam whistle, signifying shift endings and beginnings, and had, like all the town's inhabitants, learned to keep track of time through this regular sound. This was no usual short signal, however, but a continuous, repetitious shrieking.

Lang dropped her hand and jumped up.

'My God, there's been an accident.'

He grabbed his hat, and together they ran outside, to the corner, and into the main street. Houses and shops alike were spilling out their occupants, the baker white with flour, the farrier in his leather apron, the postmistress, a carpenter still carrying his hammer — all the tradespeople, and from the side streets, housewives in cotton dresses and shawls, pale and anxious.

'What has happened?'

Lang confronted Constable Price as the policeman, buttoning up his jacket, hurried out of the station.

'A cave-in down in the lower level. Excuse me, Mr Firebrace.'

Driving his buggy, Dr Jago pushed through the crowd thronging across the roadway, the nursing sister who managed the town's small new hospital sitting at his side, prim in her cape and starched cap. As miners off shift, clattering in their heavy boots, their peculiarly look-alike Cornish faces strained, jostled through the flow towards the frames and buildings of Western Consolidated, Amy felt an arm through hers, and saw Hannah at her side.

'We'd best go home, honey. We can do nothing.'

This was sense, and yet how strong was the urge to remain with the scurrying, anxious crowd. Ahead, they heard a woman scream, and go on screaming. The Methodist minister hurried past. She was a miner's wife, one of his flock, bereaved on what had started as an ordinary working day. Lang's fingers touched Amy's cheek briefly.

'I'll see you later,' he promised, and she went back with Hannah, walking downhill towards the business part of town, leaving the crowd behind while the whistle still blared its plea for help.

'I should feel so happy, but now this dreadful thing has happened! I — oh, that poor woman!' It was all mixed inside of her, shock with joy. 'Hannah, Lang asked me to marry him, and I've accepted.'

Hannah stopped dead, wrenching Amy's arm a little as she did so, her sloe eyes flickering with anger.

'You're joking! What about the mine? I didn't think he'd go so far . . . '

Amy was both aghast and furious.

'We happen to be in love,' she snapped, and hurried on alone, leaving Hannah to stare after her, lips tight and eyes still angry.

The day, which had started with annoyance, then moved into a high state of bliss before plunging into tragedy, had not finished.

'Captain' Polkinghorne, works manager at the mine, took a team of men with lanterns and a windlass and digging implements and air-pumping equipment, to a certain spot in the old police paddock. There, he knew, was an abandoned shaft which might, in the desperation which now gripped rescuers seeking to save men still trapped below, offer access to the deepest tunnels of the Western Consolidated.

At the bottom of the shaft, in a puddle of seepage, lay the broken body of Jane Kestle, the Dolly Varden hat she had stolen still pinned to the bloodstained hair. She had not died in the fall. She had been shot through the back of the neck.

14

That was Tuesday. On Thursday morning, the inquest into the death of Jane Agnes Kestle was held in the courthouse, with the town's other and senior doctor, Linus Milligan, presiding as coroner. On the same day, the inquest into the death of Thomas Peter Johns, miner, was to be heard, and with two more bodies recovered on the previous afternoon and another man still missing, it seemed as if Dr Milligan's Friday would be likewise occupied.

The town was stunned by the tragedy. Accidental death was never far away for a miner, for skill, combined with a degree of good fortune, usually protected him, but rock, weakened somewhere between the roof of the tunnel and the overburden, had shifted without warning, and this is what had happened far down in the Western Consolidated.

In these circumstances, Jane's death was almost a sideshow, away from the mainstream of disaster. A relief fund had been opened, with Langdon Firebrace leading the contributors by donating a hundred pounds and his sister the same. Before Wednesday was out, telegraphed information arrived from Melbourne stating that an appeal for money to assist the widows and their families had been launched.

Wednesday morning, early, Amy went to her father's desk and felt in the secret compartment. The gun had gone. Constable Price, harried by the snowballing of events, had interviewed Hannah and herself the previous evening. So, Jane's death was the culmination of a string of odd happenings, and Amy lay coldly in her bed, trying to chase away the morbid conclusions which crowded in about her.

Had Lang found it necessary to rid himself of Jane Kestle before asking her, Amy, to marry him?

No, no, and no!

Except for the accident, Jane's body may not have been found for weeks. It would have been concluded that she had run away with her small amount of booty, and no proper search made.

Then Amy, about midnight, remembered the pistol. Constable Price had said that it was thought that Jane had been shot with a small-bore weapon, probably a pistol.

Hannah always slept late, and even such a disturbing occurrence as the death of a household servant did not shorten her slumbers.

'The pistol's gone,' Amy announced, and Hannah's deepset eyes, heavy under her lace nightcap, blinked.

'Oh, that,' she said, turning to sleep again. 'I took it. With all these things happening, I thought it a good idea to keep it handy.'

The same day she received the reply to her letter about Edmund Felstead's address book. Mr Parker had made careful enquiries, but it was definitely not amongst those papers taken from her father's house after his death.

Had McIntyre taken it? He had written to her half-sister Hannah, presumably using an address taken from the book, but not to her, unless Elspeth had confiscated the letter.

It was always the same. When she began thinking of the enigmas connected with her father's death, she always came back to McIntyre.

The courthouse was a squarish timber building entered through a roofed porch, built in the early sixties when there was still some doubt as to whether it was worth erecting a more solid structure. The courtroom was set out traditionally, but although it is an axiom that justice must be seen to be done, the public desirous of viewing proceedings had little room at its disposal in these small premises.

For the inquest, chairs had been brought from elsewhere to seat the bereaved, and three plain wooden benches had to suffice for others.

Dr Jago gave the medical evidence. Jane Agnes Kestle had been shot through the back of the neck at very close range with a small-bore firearm, probably a pistol, although as the bullet had passed straight through, there was little chance of establishing this definitely. She would have died almost immediately, and it was his opinion that she had been killed elsewhere and later thrown down into the shaft. She was also in the early stages of pregnancy.

This last announcement was met with loud sobbing from Mrs Arthur Kestle, who, encased in black, sat next to the Morcan Kestles, who were still and stony-faced, their hard-fought-for respectability crumbled by one child in their brood of ten.

John Polkinghorne, the mine manager, wearing a black armband on the sleeve of his frock coat as a mark of respect to those who had died in the accident, briefly outlined the circumstances in which Jane's body had been found. At the inquest following this one, he would have again to give evidence, and twice or three times after that. For him, it was a hard and distressing ordeal: he had known many of his miners and their families for years, back into the times when they had all been employed in the copper mines in South Australia.

At the same time, he was anxious to be back at the mine. Even as he awaited his turn here at the court, the leader of one of the miners' teams had brought him unbelievable tidings. Jared Trembath, last of the trapped men, was alive. They had heard his tap beyond the rock fall, and 'Captain' Polkinghorne, a devout man, prayed that they would be in time.

Oscar Howarth sat on one of the forms provided for the public, leaning forward the better to hear, and jotting down notes from time to time. To Amy, falteringly answering the questions put to her by the clerk, his attention was unnerving. From his own seat, next to the one she had vacated, Lang Firebrace smiled at her encouragingly, and Hannah, a bird-of-paradise amidst the sad blackbirds of the dead girl's family, looked down at her gloves. Her whole demeanour stated plainly that she was here by accident, and pulled into it by circumstances beyond her control. George Ross, the solicitor who had been retained by Lang Firebrace to protect Amy's interest, looked unutterably bored.

Yes, she had hired Jane Kestle immediately upon moving into the house left to her by her father. Actually, the hiring had been arranged by Mrs Arthur Kestle, and she had had little personal knowledge of either Jane's friends or habits.

Mrs Arthur Kestle immediately burst into noisy tears and the coroner had to rap with his gavel before quiet was restored.

'It is the understanding of this court that you, or someone in your house, were the victim of a number of unpleasant pranks subsequent to your taking up residence there?'

'Yes,' said Amy.

'You reported some of these incidents, including the poisoning of your dog, to the police?'

'Yes.'

'Did you have any opinion as to who had perpetrated those actions?'

Every face in the stuffy little courtroom was turned towards her. A blowfly buzzed against one of the windows, knocking its maggot-heavy body against the glass, loud in the expectant silence. Mrs Morcan Kestle, Mary Anne Kestle who worked for the Firebraces, Mr Morcan Kestle, and the rest of the numerous tribe, stared at her, eyes hard with blame. Hannah had removed a glove and was fiddling with her rings, Lang Firebrace smiled at Amy again, and Oscar Howarth was alert.

'No,' said Amy, and was aware of the disappointment. Am I lying, she thought, her mouth dry.

'According to Constable Price, you were under the impression that these pranks were directed against you?'

'For a while, yes.'

'Why, Miss Felstead?'

Now George Ross intervened. This was a coroner's inquiry, neither a preliminary hearing nor a trial. Miss Felstead's thoughts in this matter were completely irrelevant. She had been persuaded, innocently on her part, into employing a young girl of poor local reputation.

There was an outraged collective cry from the Kestles. Jane's parents had long since washed their hands of her, but that was a private matter and public airing of Jane's failings reflected on them all. The gavel was hammered again, and the clerk, consulting the statement which Amy had given the police, asked another question.

Miss Felstead had said that the deceased had left without giving notice, but after a slight disagreement with herself. Could she enlarge?

'Jane frequently quarrelled with my sister's servant. I told her that she must try to keep the peace,' returned Amy, trying to sound confident.

'You did not know that Jane Kestle was pregnant?'

'Of course not.'

That was all, but the next witness was a surprise. Mary Anne Kestle went rather red in the face as she took the oath. Sitting down again alongside Lang Firebrace, Amy saw that he too was astonished, and he whispered in her ear.

'That's odd. She didn't mention it to *us*.'

Mary Anne recovered her nerve, and tossed her black-bonneted head with a certain defiance as she looked about the court.

'Miss Kestle,' said the clerk, gently, 'you made a statement to Constable Price yesterday regarding your sister, Jane Agnes Kestle. You said, 'Jane told me she was going to be married and that the town would be abuzz over it. Jane told me when she was married, there were those who looked down on her now and bossed her about who'd be singing a different tune before long!' '

Lang Firebrace's hand closed over Amy's and squeezed it, firmly and warmly.

'Little liar,' he said, almost under his breath, but virtually every head in the courtroom jerked up, and Oscar Howarth in particular fairly bristled with interest.

The coroner, leaning forward with fascination, asked a question direct.

'Miss Kestle, do you have any idea whom this man might be?'

Mary Anne glanced about the court, her gaze resting for a moment on her employer, and then she shook her head, almost regretfully.

'No,' she said, 'it was all a secret, like. But he was a real gent, she said. Jack Beaton always said . . . '

'Yes?'

The young woman flushed scarlet again.

'He said — he works for Mr Firebrace like I do — that he'd kill Jane before he saw her married to anyone else.'

'Rubbish,' muttered Langdon Firebrace. 'Only the drink talking. Jack can't hold his liquor.'

'Is Mr Beaton in court?'

Constable Price had to admit that John Beaton was not. In fact, John Beaton had left early the previous day to travel to the Riverina District up in New South Wales to

179

collect some sheep Mr Firebrace had recently purchased. He had queried Mr Firebrace regarding this, and Mr Firebrace had told him that there had been some trouble between two blackfellows he employed and John Beaton, owing to Beaton's brother having been killed by blacks up near Palmerston on the Overland Telegraph line. He had chosen Beaton for the errand to give him a chance to 'cool off'.

Dr Milligan, the coroner, appeared rather annoyed, but he adjusted his spectacles, glanced across at the clock, and gave his verdict without further consideration. Jane Agnes Kestle had died as the result of a gunshot wound unlawfully afflicted by a person or persons unknown.

Outside, the Kestles stalked past the group comprising Langdon Firebrace, Amy, Hannah and George Ross.

'Don't take any notice of them,' advised Eric Jago, smiling kindly at Amy as he joined them for a few moments before returning to the courthouse to give evidence at the second inquest. 'Jane had charted her course long before you came out here, Miss Felstead.'

The solicitor, too, had other duties, and was eager to be off. Before leaving, however, he had something to say.

'Our police out here aren't altogether fools,' he stated, addressing Amy. 'They'll soon catch the culprit.'

Hannah erected her frilly sunshade, for the day was warming up in the rapid fashion of these latitudes once winter had passed.

'There can't be many in the district who own hand guns,' she remarked, but followed this up with a warning look at her half-sister, plainly because of the weapon they had found in their father's desk. 'This isn't the Wild West, where everyone is armed.'

'I could name a dozen,' said Lang Firebrace. 'Not that the guns are used, but most of the older hands bought pistols or revolvers a few years back when we had bushrangers in the area.'

Now that the ordeal of giving evidence with the baleful eyes of the Kestles glaring at her was past, Amy began to assemble her ideas. Jane Kestle, who had bragged about the 'gent' who loved her and, presumably, had made her pregnant, had died, and a few hours later Lang Firebrace had asked her, Amy, to marry him. Neither could she forget the way Mary Anne Kestle had looked at him during the inquest.

All the suspicions, smothered temporarily by kisses and the euphoria of infatuation, came back in gathered force.

'I'll walk with you back to the school,' he offered, while Hannah, with a gay wave of

181

the hand, turned and tripped off homewards, her colourful appearance drawing more than one appreciative glance and remark from nearby loungers.

'I can go on my own, thank you,' said Amy.

But, he had her arm, and they walked away from the courthouse into the main street, past the police station, past the shops, and towards Mrs Stacey's school. Oscar Howarth, in the bar of The Commercial for a quick reviver before the second inquest, watched them, the anxious, pale girl, and the tall, handsome man with the easy, good-humoured arrogance.

Envy stirred sourly inside Oscar Howarth. He was forty-six years of age. The dreams of fame and fortune which had brought him to the Fish Creek Diggings, as they were then known, eighteen years earlier had dwindled into an unwilling acceptance of the truth that he was stuck here in this misnamed township probably for the rest of his life. He had arrived with little more than a few pence, and if the town dwindled away as it could without the assurance of continued mining, he would be buried without leaving much more than a few pence in his bank account.

There had been no inherited wealth for

182

him, to ease his way and cover his sins and make the girls set their caps at him. His wife had left him for a weightlifter with a travelling circus. She said he drank too much.

Now, why had Firebrace whipped young Beaton away like that? Because he thought Beaton was guilty and wanted to protect him? Or . . . did Beaton know too much?

Oscar Howarth tossed down the rest of his drink, and it warmed its way down his gullet. He considered having another, and regretfully put aside the idea. Duty called, and his Cornish readers would expect a fairly faithful account of the inquest into the death of one of their kind. Stepping out into the street, he noted that Firebrace and the girl had turned the corner into the street where Mrs Stacey's school stood, and at the same time he glanced diagonally across the roadway to his office. That smart and dashing piece, Miss Hannah Felstead, was just going inside.

He did not hesitate. In the light of present circumstances, there was nothing more that he wanted than a quiet chat with the older Felstead woman who, rumour said, had been left out of Edmund's will. Hannah was telling Albert Hancock, his employee, that she would return later as Howarth entered,

183

and once again the newspaper owner was impressed by her resemblance to Edmund Felstead. It was all there, the corsair look, the hint of dark and uncertain blood, Red Indian perhaps, the whole air of one used to picking a way through dangerous and uncharted waters.

'Albert,' he said to the youth, who, although officially a printer, sometimes doubled as a journalist, 'I want you to go to the courthouse. You can handle the inquest into Charlie Trebilcock's death. You're a Cousin Jack. You understand 'em better than I do.'

Hannah, as soon as the lad had left, sat down on the visitor's chair and smiled at Howarth.

'I think,' she said, 'that it's time you and I had a little talk.'

Howarth bolted the door and sat down himself. Then, on an impulse, he opened a drawer and pulled out a flask and two glasses, and Hannah smiled again.

'I can see,' she said, 'that you and I are going to understand one another.'

★ ★ ★

'Please, I want to be alone for a little while,' protested Amy.

'Why?' demanded the man, aggressively. 'Two days ago you agreed to marry me.'

'Lang, I'm sorry. I let myself be carried away. I must have more time to think about it.'

On the previous Sunday, she had seen how quickly anger could darken his face. It was as if the smiling mask had been snatched away and replaced by one saturnine and scowling.

'Oh, do you now? The truth is you think I killed Jane Kestle because I got her into trouble and she threatened to tell you that I'd talked her into terrorising you, isn't that so?' He was in a rage, kept in check only because the place was in public view, and the hand which had taken her arm so lightly now gripped tightly so that his powerful fingers dug into her flesh. 'Or has that shady sister of yours been influencing you? It's as plain as the nose on your face that she's not pleased at the idea of you marrying me.'

'My sister has nothing to do with it. And it would please me if you spoke of her in a more respectful manner.' Not for all the world would she have admitted that she had serious doubts about Hannah herself. 'Lang, I cannot rush into marriage. I must have time to think.'

It sounded rational, but she knew that

185

she was lying. More than anything else, she wanted to marry Lang Firebrace. She was almost frantically in love with him, but at the same time she was frightened of the doubts which refused to be dismissed.

'Well, tell me. What exactly does your sister want? She didn't come all the way from America to look at the scenery. She's an adventuress, and the quicker she leaves, the better I'll be pleased. Frankly, she's not quite the sort of family I want.'

'Oh.' She had pulled free, and it was only with an effort of self-control that she did not stamp her foot. 'I dare say you'd like to see her go. I'd be completely without support then. Hannah came because she believed that she had a claim to the Royal Edward, and she has accepted the fact that she hasn't in good grace. Which is more than can be said for certain other people I know.'

'Ah, the mine. We're coming back to the hub of it. Haven't you ever heard of fool's gold?'

He was speaking to empty air. She had gone, running the last hundred yards to the school, biting back tears, and desperately trying to compose herself before facing Mrs Stacey and the children.

Dimly, she knew that men were hurrying

past. One spoke to her, quietly but proudly.

'He's alive. We got him out alive.'

Four families in Firebrace were in mourning, and their sorrow had to temper the joy of others.

15

Amy's day continued on the downgrade. Her pupils seemed determined to be as stupid and refractory as children could be, and as she walked home, feeling utterly miserable, she encountered Allison Firebrace. Langdon's sister was elegantly austere in a navy blue riding habit, for she had chosen to come into town on horseback, and she cut Amy dead.

Fifty yards further along, Dr Jago's outfit drew up alongside the white and trembling Amy.

'Would you care for a lift?' he asked, and although it would be for no more than a few hundred yards, she accepted gratefully. It seemed to her, then, that the doctor was the only stable person with whom she had become acquainted in this town.

He did not alter. He was always the same, calm, rather brusque, and if he had fits of temper, he kept them out of public sight.

'You mustn't let Miss Firebrace upset you,' he admonished, as Amy sat silent and fuming.

'Upset? None of that family upset me,' she replied.

'I think you've good reason to be upset. She'll do her best to stop her brother marrying you. Not because you're you, but because it'll overturn her applecart.'

This so echoed what Hannah had said on the previous Sunday that she half-turned to him in involuntary surprise.

'So don't let her do it,' he continued.

'I'm not marrying Mr Firebrace, Dr Jago,' she returned, primly. 'You have been misinformed.'

Outside her house, he helped her down.

'Miss Felstead,' he said, gravely, 'you mustn't allow yourself to think that Lang had any connection with poor Jane Kestle. I doubt whether he'd ever seen her, except in the distance. I dare say someone's told you about the lady in Ballarat — well, forget that, too. It's been over for a year. And I might say that she really is a lady. Lang's too proud to cheapen himself chasing after servant girls.'

'I wish,' she said, acidly, turning away with a swish of skirts, 'that everyone would mind their own business.'

It did not help to hear the doctor, usually so serious in his manner, laugh quite loudly.

Polly, who must have been watching, opened the door for her with the information that Miss Hannah was in the parlour, but

Amy went straight to her room and sat down for five minutes to recover. The only conceivable reason Dr Jago could have to reassure her about Langdon Firebrace was that what he said was true. For the flimsiest reasons, she had allowed herself to be carried away emotionally, and quarrel with a man with whom she was very much in love.

Yet, after she had washed her face and tidied her hair, she saw that Dr Jago was not as disinterested as he appeared on the surface. He had every reason to keep on Lang's good side. His daughter, born of a Firebrace mother, was in the family's clutches, and only by retaining Lang's friendship could he hope to obtain control of Avis without becoming implicated in a battle as destructive to the child as to the other parties involved.

Hannah was passing the time with a game of patience, and her half-sister caught the whiff of spirits on her breath. She was not in any way affected by liquor, but this fresh evidence of Hannah's inclinations disturbed Amy.

Lang, however hateful the admission, was right. Hannah *was* shady. Nothing about her past or background had been satisfactorily explained. She seemed to have plenty of money, but had come here hotfooted on the trail of wealth. Her clothes, expensive and beautifully made, were flattering, but not quite those of a lady.

'I found a woman to come in and do the cleaning and some of the cooking,' announced Hannah, contemplating a card before carefully placing it.

'It won't be a permanent job,' said Amy, sitting down wearily. 'Hannah, I'm going back to England.'

'Going back?' Hannah's ear-rings glinted as she moved her head quickly. 'Honey, what on earth do you mean? You're going to marry Langdon Firebrace.'

'No, I'm not. I've changed my mind.'

Hannah's face was blank as she considered this, and then she laughed, shortly.

'Well, that is a surprise, I must say. I thought he'd quite swept you off your feet. Honey, does that mean you're going to try to keep the mine for us, after all?'

'Us?' echoed Amy. She was drained down to her last ounce of vitality.

'Honey, if you stand any chance of winning the case, I know you'll remember that I'm as much our father's daughter as you are.' As she spoke, Hannah delicately placed another card. Cards on the table, thought Amy.

'I'm prepared,' continued Hannah, not looking up, 'to back you up financially if

191

you'll recognise my claim.'

'I'm not interested in the wretched mine! I'm going to accept whatever the settlement of Todd Firebrace's debt to our father works out to be. I want to go back Home. I'm frightened, Hannah.' She drew a deep breath, and voiced her suspicions. 'How do I know that you really are my half-sister? You do resemble my father, but you could be a distant relative.'

Her game completed, Hannah grabbed up the cards and shuffled them with almost professional skill.

'Oh!' she declared. 'Oh, and oh! Really, my little sister, you've taken quite a while to realise that you've taken me on my word right from the very start. Now listen to me. I am your half-sister, and I have papers to prove it, my birth certificate, and that of my brother, and his death certificate, poor boy. But they're not here with me, honey. They're in safe keeping with the American consul in Melbourne. Something I've learnt, honey, is that it pays to be friendly with the American consul wherever I go.'

And Hannah leaned back in her chair and smiled, her tongue just moistening the inside of her lips.

'I think whether or not I try to hold the

mine is up to me,' cried Amy, 'and I want to go home.'

'We'll see,' said Hannah. 'If we could find our Mr McIntyre, we'd know better what to do.'

It was as if Amy had not spoken. Hannah had taken control. She knew what she wanted and was determined to get it.

'I think he's dead,' she said, numbly. Until this moment, she had not thought of it, but it seemed as good an explanation of McIntyre's complete disappearance as any.

'No. The more I think of it, the more I wonder whether he was Jane's gentleman. He could be hiding somewhere in the hills. I'm told there are plenty of old shacks and huts scattered about through the valleys.'

'But there's no point in it, Hannah. Whatever happened, he'd never have the slightest chance of owning the Royal Edward.'

Polly entered and announced that their dinner was ready, at the same time conveying her disgust at being lowered to the status of a general servant. As Hannah led the way to the dining-room, silken skirts whispering, it came to Amy, coldly and clearly. If something happened to her, Hannah was her nearest blood kin.

After school the following day, Amy made it her business to call at the police station.

Constable Price, with whom she had had her previous dealings, was absent, but the sergeant listened to her request as to any knowledge he might have of the whereabouts of Samuel McIntyre.

'Now, Miss Felstead, why should you be wanting to know such a thing?' he asked, in a voice thick with the bogs of Derry. 'He wasn't the sort of fellow a young lady the likes of yourself should be wanting to know.'

'He knew my father. There are one or two things he could tell me — us, I mean. He did write to my half-sister, but she's heard no more of him.'

'Not to be wondered at, Miss Felstead. Victoria was too hot for him. There was a little matter of promoting a goldmine which didn't seem to exist up there in Castlemaine, Forest Creek as they used to call it before they got the sense to give it a good Irish name.'

'I didn't know . . . I . . . ' She was floundering. 'What was he like? A gentleman?'

'Sam McIntyre?' Sergeant Riordan pursed his lips. 'Well, there's gentlemen and gentlemen, you might say. Some that really are, whether they're born to high station or not. Sam now, he was a colonial lad, and they say his old dad was transported to Tasmania. He could put it on when it suited him, depending on company, or talk as rough as a shearer's cook if he was mixing with that sort. He lived on his wits, Miss Felstead, and if he shows his face here again, half the town'll be after him to collect money owing 'em.'

'Do you think that he could be in the district?'

Sergeant Riordan laughed.

'Now, why should he be coming back here? He's found fresh pastures, Miss Felstead, somewhere his wicked ways aren't known. I know what's worrying you. It's this grievous business of Jane Kestle. You're not to worry about it. We've our own ideas on what happened. We're checking on everyone that young baggage was ever friendly with, including those in Ballarat. We're not as smart to look at as those city detectives, Miss Felstead, but we'll be catching up with that scoundrel before he knows what's happened to him.'

If Sergeant Riordan had known the contents of that article penned by Oscar Howarth, now snugly in a mailbag on its way to Melbourne, he would have felt neither benign nor confident.

16

In later years, a happily married woman with a young family to occupy her attention and a good husband to protect her, Amy would occasionally look back on those days in Firebrace with wonderment, see the pretty, confused, unhappy girl as almost a stranger, more akin to a character in a novel than her present contented and somewhat matronly self.

He had made no move, and she deliberately avoided those places where she was likely to encounter him. Hannah stayed on, revealing nothing about her plans, but hiring a horse from the stables and going out riding on fine afternoons. The elder sister received several letters that week, but did not reveal the contents. For Amy, this was a week without letters, nothing from Mr Parker, and nothing from England. The latter was a disappointment explained by a notice in the post office window. The mail steamer *Goliath* had caught fire whilst in Port Said and the mail in her hold had been destroyed.

The most exciting event, and the most talked about outside the discussions over the town's new name, was that Firebrace post office had dealt with its first overseas cable, all the way from England under the ocean, past Timor, to Palmerston, and then down the O.T. Line to Adelaide and across to Melbourne and west back to Firebrace. Fittingly, it was to Miss and Mr Firebrace, from their sister Lady Harkness, the one who had married a baronet.

This made the whole town glow. It had been linked to the outside world within a few days of the O.T. Line going into full operation, and Amy, rather gallingly, had to show her pupils the path of the cable on the wall map. She had to pretend that the onion which had been cut in two for nature study, the next period, was responsible for her eyes watering as she visualised handsome Langdon Firebrace and his horrid sister poring excitedly over their cable.

Yet, even when one is frightened, lonely, lovesick and aware that one has probably made the worst mistake of one's life, days pass by quite quickly.

'As soon as Mr Parker lets me know if there's enough money in my account to pay my fare back to England, I'm off,' stated Amy, and saw this as a good opportunity to bring matters to a head. 'This house will be sold, Hannah. There'll be no reason for you to stay.'

'Don't worry, honey. I'm off to Melbourne Monday. I'm going to see a lawyer of my own.'

'Oh, have half the wretched estate, and be done with it!' Amy was almost in tears. 'I don't care any more. I only want to be away from this wretched place. I'll go back to England and marry Charlie Henthorne and try to forget everything about — about . . . ' Her voice trailed off, as Hannah smiled at her knowingly.

'So,' murmured the other, 'that is why little Amy came all the way to Australia. To escape from a man. What was he like? Old and ugly?'

'Certainly not. Charlie's about thirty, and not bad-looking and quite rich.'

How odd it was that Charlie Henthorne, whose suit had so distressed her only a few months ago, now seemed solid and desirable in this chaotic world.

'He's really very nice,' she added.

'You seem to be very fortunate in the men you meet,' commented Hannah, and she made no attempt to hide the cutting edge in her voice. 'And at least, honey, you'll never have the nasty little suspicion that he killed a girl to get her out of the way so that he could marry you.'

Monday, thought Amy, gritting her teeth. On Monday she'll be going, and I don't care in the least what she does after that. She may be my half-sister, but I do not like her.

Mrs Stacey told her in the morning that Mr Polkinghorne, whose two daughters were pupils at the school, had sent a note asking that Miss Felstead call at his office up at the Western Consolidated that afternoon.

'Mr Polkinghorne, the manager at the mine?' Amy's voice reflected her surprise, as much at the way in which the request had been relayed as at the invitation. She knew him by sight, and, of course, he had been a witness at the inquest into Jane Kestle's death, but she was at a loss to understand why he should wish to see her. Surely, if he had information about Jane Kestle, he would hand it on directly to the police.

'Yes, my dear. Now, don't look so worried. I'm sure that he has no cause to complain about your work here at the school.' The widow smiled in that warm way of hers, and once again Amy felt a deep flow of gratitude for the constant kindness Mrs Stacey had shown towards her. 'Mr Polkinghorne is a very proper and respectable man, and I'm sure that he felt that, as he isn't acquainted with you, it was more correct to send the message through me.'

The Western Consolidated was about a quarter of a mile from the school, uphill all the way, and as the day was warm, with spring hardening now into summer and the grass browning from its soft, almost English green, the girl felt a little sticky and weary by the time she reached the gates. Here, the thudding of the battery was all-pervasive, and Amy wondered how the tenants of the tiny cottages close by could endure the noise. Mr Polkinghorne's office was pointed out to her by the gatekeeper, and as she walked carefully across ground rough with shale and rubble, she paused to pick up a fistsized piece of rock glistening with a golden band.

'Now, Miss Felstead, it's against the law for an unauthorised person to remove stone from a mining lease!'

'Captain' Polkinghorne came from his office, a small building in its own right, set a distance from the main poppet heads and crushing plant. He was a stocky man wearing his managerial frock coat open over a waistcoat embellished with a heavy watch-chain, carrying with him an air of responsibility and authority. Nevertheless, as he spoke, straightfaced, there was a twinkle in the blue eyes.

'That's pyrites you're looking at,' he

continued. 'It's much brighter looking than gold. What we call fool's gold. Oh, keep it. I'll turn a blind eye.'

She allowed herself to be escorted into the office, and then, as the tall man who had been seated near the window arose, her heart thumped so that blood coloured her cheeks and threatened to choke her voice.

'You know Mr Firebrace already, I believe,' said Polkinghorne with unconscious understatement. 'This concerns both of you, and it concerns the whole mining community here.'

Amy and Langdon Firebrace carefully ignored each other, and gave all their attention to the grey-bearded mine manager.

'I've heard a lot of talk the past couple o' weeks about opening up the Royal Edward. There's elements here who're determined on it, and I understand there's some ready to pool money to help Miss Felstead go ahead. Now, I want to make it plain, for once and for all, that mine's no good. The Jack o' Lantern it used to be called, and a reg'lar will-o'-the-wisp it turned out to be for those who invested their money. Your father knew that, Mr Firebrace. He had a thorough survey made.'

'I know,' nodded the other man, with a cool glance towards Amy.

201

'The trouble is, Miss Felstead,' said Polkinghorne, 'that the McIntyre fellow talked your father into believing a false assay he'd written up on paper belonging to a firm he'd worked for until they found out his ways and sacked him. I spoke to Mr Felstead just a few hours before he died and convinced him that the Royal Edward wasn't any good. That's the absolute truth, whatever they're saying about Mr Firebrace thinking more of his own interests than the town's.'

'Thank you,' said Amy, quietly, for she could do nothing but believe this blunt, practical Cornishman. She looked down at the piece of stone she still held. Fool's gold, how appropriate. 'Could you write to my solicitors in Melbourne, and inform them of the real position?'

'Certainly, Miss Felstead. Mining's my life and, believe me, I'd have liked to see another mine opened up here to keep us miners in work when the Consolidated is played out.'

Langdon Firebrace excused himself, and she wrote out Parker's address before going outside. He was waiting for her.

'All right,' she said, defiantly, 'you've been right all along, and I owe you an apology.'

She wanted nothing but to bolt off home and indulge in a bout of weeping over her

202

own folly. What hateful stuff gold is, she thought. It made me think the worst of this fine, decent man who offered me his name, because all the time I hoped that the Royal Edward would make me enormously rich. I believed him capable of the most detestable plotting and . . . of murder.

But he smiled, and took her arm, and, as if by magic, everything was all right. She told him that Hannah was leaving, and he laughed.

'That's a coincidence. Allison's off to England, you know. I wrote to our sister there months ago suggesting that she invite Allison for a prolonged visit, and the invitation arrived by cable. Allison's a clever and talented woman, Amy, but she's wasting her life away carrying a grudge. Eric's marrying again, and it's all working out rather well.'

'Dr Jago is marrying?'

'Yes. The lady who runs our little hospital.'

As he said, everything was working out well. Hannah and her devious schemes were removing themselves, Miss Allison and her uncertain temper were away to England, little Avis was going to her papa, and niggling obstacles had been cleared away as if by magic.

For a little while, on the high sunny path

overlooking the township, with the machinery and buildings of the Western Consolidated like toys below, she could forget the unsolved puzzle of the practical jokes and Jane Kestle's death, and McIntyre's part in the drama, and whether old Jimmy had heard a pistol shot inside the Royal Edward when her father had died.

'The coach is late,' remarked Lang. 'See, over there, just coming out from the trees.'

She could barely see it, for she did not have his gift of long sight, but by straining her vision she could perceive the coach and its team pulling out of that last dip, obscured partly by trees, about a mile to the east of Firebrace.

17

In that same coach, Detective Glover shifted wearily for the thousandth time and decided again that he would be glad when the railway extended further west. As far as he could ascertain, the road had not improved since those days when the Firebrace area had been known as Fish Creek Diggings and he had been a raw young constable trying to keep law and order amidst a mixed lot of miners who disliked police as much as they loathed the Chinese who were at that time arriving in large numbers.

That was fifteen years ago, and he had long settled into his own particular niche as a detective attached to the headquarters of the Victoria Police in Melbourne. Rapid promotion through the ranks had not come his way: like many clever and worthy men of his time, he was crippled by lack of formal education. As well, he occasionally annoyed his superiors by a stubborn determination to do things his own way. Observant, shrewd, and with a memory for faces and incidents which had brought many a criminal to court, he was one of the smartest men in the force.

Ordinarily, Detective Glover would not have been sent up bush to investigate a murder, for local men were usually competent enough and sufficiently well versed in local conditions to solve such cases. What had prompted a near-eruption in the chief commissioner's office on Wednesday morning was a report in *The Age*, Melbourne's most radical newspaper.

The Age was always ready to fight the establishment, whilst the chief commissioner, a good enough man in his own way, was more at home in society drawing-rooms than in more commonplace surroundings.

Poor teenaged Jane Kestle, with her sleazy dreams of romance ending in murder, had thus become the trigger which could set off a political bomb. Allegations of police inefficiency, or, as the special correspondent bluntly hinted, police favouritism towards those whom it feared to offend, were always good material for a debate in the lower House.

The Firebrace police, it was alleged, had lagged in their duty while the town's womenfolk, many in deepest mourning following the recent mine tragedy, walked in fear of their lives. The callous killing of a young servant girl had followed a reign of terror against a household comprising helpless women, and, needless to say, the police, disregarding the sinister undertone of impending maniacy, had done nothing to find the perpetrator. Rumour pointed in one direction, but just as there are places where angels fear to tread, policemen are sometimes fearful of tipping the seat of power.

Of course, Glover was not briefed by anyone as august as a police commissioner, but his immediate superior put it to him frankly.

'Get to the bottom of it. The area's pretty orderly as a rule, but the commissioner's frightened that his neck's at stake over this.'

Glover went to *The Age* offices, not through the front door, but round to the back where the printing works were located. He knew a compositor there, who managed, through an office boy, to find out to whom money was due out Firebrace way. The special correspondent was one Oscar Howarth, editor of the Firebrace newspaper. Detective Glover pondered whether Mr Howarth had been prompted by envy or by avarice. Public spiritedness, in Glover's opinion, was a scarce commodity.

In Ballarat, he had made certain enquiries, learning that Jane Kestle worked there for a while as a chambermaid in a hotel. She'd left quite suddenly. No reason. Just gave her notice and left, said the proprietor. Not that he was sorry. She was a baggage, and he'd employed her in the first place as a favour to the Methodist minister in Firebrace who was related to his wife. To give the girl her due, she was a hard worker, but there had been complaints that she had been seen coming out of bedrooms where she'd had no cause to be. He was thinking of sacking her when she'd upped and left.

Having thus laid a small foundation for his investigations, Detective Glover endured the coach trip west. He did not bother with scenery, but sat stolidly, a stout man whose impending baldness was hidden by his bowler hat. His fellow passengers may have assumed that he was dozing, but he was riding, in memory, through the country about the old Fish Creek Diggings.

There were the ranges to the north and east, with the town on the first slopes, so that the whole place was on a slant, and Fish Creek, a nice stream before the diggers ruined it, acting as a border on the west. To the south, the country flattened out, dotted with lakes and swamps where the blacks, what was left of them, poor wretches, had still hunted and fished. To the south-west was that striking group of ranges, the Grampians.

He had ridden into the passes a few times, seeking malefactors, and the Grampians had always scared him, with their great sheets of serrated rock rearing thousands of feet into the air, the dense forests climbing up through clefts and valleys, and the snowstorms whipping about the peaks in winter. A black tracker employed by the police had told him that the spirit who had founded his people back in the beginning of time had come to earth in the Grampians, and Sergeant Glover thought it likely.

After arranging the area in his mind, he took to studying his nine fellow passengers. There were three women returning from a shopping expedition to Ballarat, two commercial travellers of the brash variety who dallied with chambermaids, a bank clerk, two middle-aged graziers, and the new chum.

Out here for colonial experience, thought Glover, with a pocketful of introductions and his relatives hoping that bush life'll knock some sense into him. He wondered what use colonial experience would be back Home. This one was really going to find things hard when he took his place amongst the men on a sheep or cattle run. A tall, slender young man of about thirty, he had the ruddy sea-voyage complexion of the recent arrival which caused immigrants to be nicknamed pomegranates. Or at least that which was visible under carefully barbered dundreary whiskers, leaving the chin bare, was ruddy. A monocle stuck into one eye completed an appearance of fatuousness. His comments brought a mixture of toleration and contempt from his fellow passengers.

'I say, Melbourne actually has gaslight. Thought there'd be jolly old kangaroos bounding along the main street.'

When the graziers had recovered sufficiently from this to ask whither the newcomer was bound, the reply interested Glover, although he sat stiff and stolid.

'Firebrace. Jolly silly name for a town. I'm engaged to marry a young lady who lives there.'

The other grazier frowned, as if going through a list of eligibles in his head.

'She's only been in the colonies a short time,' added the new chum. 'A Miss Felstead. Her late father owned a goldmine.'

'Why,' said one of the women, 'that's the name of the lady poor Jane Kestle worked for. She who was murdered dead Monday of last week.'

'Oh, I say!' The new chum was flabbergasted. 'How absolutely shocking! Always told Miss Felstead she mustn't think of it. Coming to the colonies, I mean.'

Sergeant Glover noted the glares of contempt this last earned the young man, and went on quietly listening. He heard all about Jane's flighty ways and rumoured gentleman friend who was probably the one who'd done her in, and Miss Felstead's strange sister with the black servant in tow.

Then the new chum, after a period of reflection, made the remark which brought him a definite set-down.

'I say,' he said, waving a pale gloved hand in the general direction of the distant Grampians now coming into view, 'rather like Scotland, what?'

One of the graziers, a tough old veteran who had left his native Dundee thirty-five years before to make a fortune in the new lands, uttered a snorting noise.

'I dinna recall gum trees in Scotland,' he growled, which finished that line of talk.

As he collected his bag at the Firebrace coaching depot, Glover saw the man addressed as Mr Howarth by the driver. The newspaperman gathered up two bundles of overseas papers he had been expecting, and Glover assessed him as a hard drinker who had gone a bit sour on life. He would speak to our special correspondent later.

Amy walked the length of her front garden path with the slanting rays of a setting sun bronzing her hair as she swung her hat by its ribbons. Hannah, at the door, did not catch her mood of bliss, and demanded to know where on earth she had been all this while.

'I've been out walking, with Lang.' The other's tone annoyed her, and she made to pass, but Hannah took her arm and whispered warningly.

'Well, you're a fool if you let him twist you about his little finger again. For now, you've a visitor. In the parlour.'

Incredulously, she was facing Charles Henthorne. He was solid enough, taking both her suddenly cold hands in his, and kissing her cheek gently and affectionately.

'Ah, Amy, dear girl. I've heard about your ordeal. Oh, my precious girl.' He still had her hands and was staring into her face with an intensity of emotion, almost in tears, it seemed, for he suddenly whipped his monocle from its socket, wiped it on his silk handkerchief, and replaced it whilst clearing his throat.

'What on earth are you doing here?' The question tumbled out as she tried to shake away her disbelief.

'You must have had my letter. And Elspeth said that she'd write, too. I couldn't stand being parted from you, so I took a fast steamer four and a half weeks ago. I arrived in Melbourne Wednesday, took train to Ballarat yesterday, and here I am, today.'

Amy sat weakly on the nearest chair.

'But, Charlie, I've had no letters. I believe a mail steamer was burnt out at Port Said. Perhaps . . . oh, why did you come?'

Charlie took a moment or two to ponder over this.

'Yes, of course,' he muttered. 'Burnt a couple of weeks before we passed through the canal. Didn't think . . . ' Then he recovered his usual aplomb. 'But I'm here, and from what I've heard already, a dashed good thing it'll be when I take you home to England where you belong.'

'I'm not going back to England, Charlie. Not for a while, at any rate. I do wish you hadn't come, Charlie.'

'But Elspeth said you'd changed your mind. She read out your letter. You were coming back to England to marry me. So I decided to jump the jolly old gun.'

I'm going mad, thought Amy. Quite mad. Yet it was all becoming too clear. Elspeth, always so intent on having her own way, had made it up. Then, seeing Charlie's stricken

213

expression, she softened.

'I'm so sorry, Charlie. But you've come across the world on a wild goose chase. I've met a man whom I am going to marry.'

The parlour door was not shut, and neither noticed a third party in the hallway as they worked out their personal drama. Detective Glover had been invited inside by the elder Miss Felstead, and he stood, all burly awkwardness, holding his hat in his hand, and clearing his throat to attract attention. The young man, he could see, was taking it badly.

Charles Henthorne was deathly pale and, swaying, grasped the back of a chair for support whilst an anxious Amy touched his sleeve.

'Charlie!' she cried out in alarm. 'Are you all right?'

'Of course,' he said, recovering himself valiantly. 'Dashed shock, that's all. Twelve thousand miles full of hope, y'know.'

At this moment, both realised that they were not alone, and an embarrassed Glover introduced himself.

'I say,' declared Charlie, 'you were on the coach.' He stared from Glover to Amy, and back again. 'You've come all the way from Melbourne to look into the death of Miss Felstead's servant. Dashed dreadful! Still, can't expect the old law and order out here in the wilds.'

Glover's voice was placatory.

'Not as much crime out here as you'd think, sir,' he said, but now Charlie was looking straight past him at Hannah, his mouth open in bewilderment.

'Knew I'd seen you before!' he exclaimed, thumping a palm against his forehead. 'Knew it, knew it. You're not Hannah Felstead. Oh, no, you're not. You're Anna Delacroix, the spiritualistic medium!'

18

Hannah's reaction to this dramatic accusation was unexpected. She laughed.

'My secret is out,' she admitted, and went to Amy, touching the younger woman's hair affectionately. 'I guessed that a stage performer might be a little strong for my respectable sister.'

Glover, also, was undisturbed by Charlie's bombshell.

'I've read about you, Miss Delacroix,' he said. 'I think I'm right in saying you're not actually a medium. You've an act in which you show up all the tricks mediums get up to in order to defraud gullible members of the public.'

'That's so.' Hannah's eyes were agleam with mischief, or was it malice, as she turned to Charlie. 'I've nothing to hide, Mr Henthorne. My act is well known in America and Europe.'

Amy remembered now that there had been a quite heated debate in the newspapers a year or so before between the adherents of spiritualism and the scoffers who had been impressed by Anna Delacroix's clever exposé.

216

'Mr Delacroix, my stepfather,' continued Hannah, 'is a clever amateur magician, and I learnt enough to go into business exposing other people's tricks. Our father didn't approve of me going on the stage, but I'm the independent sort. I like to make my own way, and to hell with what people say. When McIntyre's letter reached me — it was sent on from my old London address — I was finishing a season in Brussels, and I thought, why not?'

'Very interesting,' said Glover, ponderously, 'but I've come to talk to Miss Amy Felstead, and I'll need a few minutes of her time.'

He stood there stolidly, determined to have his talk whatever happened, and Amy sighed, brushing a tendril of hair back from her forehead.

'Do join us at dinner, Charlie,' she said, turning to the young man who now appeared utterly wilted. 'I'm sure we can cater for one extra.'

'No, no, thank you. Simply cannot. Too upset. Want to book my passage back to Melbourne. Tomorrow's coach, if I can.'

'But, Charlie, do stay. Surely you can stay for a few days!' Amy, who was guiltless, now felt dreadfully guilty. Poor Charlie appeared to have had as much as he could bear, and she hoped that he would not do anything foolish. She had never thought that she had meant so much to him, and she felt a mounting swell of anger against Elspeth, whose irresponsible lies had led to the poor man's fruitless journey and distress.

'I want to think things over. Don't blame you, Amy, dear girl. Swept off your feet in a strange country with all these shocking things happening. Only natural you'd want a shoulder to lean on.'

With this brave, if somewhat incoherent speech, Charlie left, and Hannah shrugged.

'There's devotion for you,' she said. 'And not a cross word. Amy, you've turned down a saint. Now, Mr Detective, what is it you want to know?'

'I'll talk to Miss Felstead alone,' said Glover, and Hannah's mouth tightened before she laughed.

'All right. I dare say Amy doesn't need a chaperone in these circumstances.' And she rustled out with some dignity.

Detective Glover, so phlegmatic as he questioned Amy and listened to her replies, was more forthcoming to Sergeant Riordan as he tucked into an excellent baked roly-poly pudding prepared by Mrs Riordan. It was just as he liked, plenty of raisins and a tangy sauce with a taste of lemons.

'Miss Amy says her sister reckons a

poltergeist played those tricks at the Felstead house,' he announced, and was secretly pleased to see the other's dumbfounded expression.

'A polter-what?' The word was strange to Riordan.

'A sort of spirit. And I reckon that Miss Hannah Felstead might know what she's talking about.'

'Spirit! Now, you're not pulling my leg, are you, Mr Glover?'

'Had a case in town a couple of years back, out Fitzroy way,' continued Glover, handing his plate across to Mrs Riordan for replenishment. 'A nice terrace house, it was, and the people in it and the neighbours was scared out of their wits. China tossed about, noises in the night, and all the rest of it.'

'Nothing like that at the Felstead house,' said Riordan, sceptically.

'Oh, yes, there was. A naughty young person who was as cunning as a hatful of monkeys. The girl at the Fitzroy house did it out of sheer devilment. I'd say someone put Jane Kestle up to it.'

'Eh? Young Jane wouldn't have touched a spider if her life had depended on it.'

'But she's from a large family. I'll bet there's a young brother or cousin she gave sixpence to so's he'd do the job.'

'And the poisoned dog?'

'More likely the person who wanted to scare the wits out of Miss Amy.'

'We're sure the tricks were against Jane, not Miss Felstead. The only one with a grudge against Miss Amy'd be Mr Firebrace, over the Royal Edward Mine, and they seem to have settled *that* between them. It doesn't make sense, Mr Glover.'

'No? We'll see.' Glover quaffed a cup of good strong tea, so laced with sugar that the flavour was lost. 'This McIntyre now, was he a good-looking fellow, likely to sweep a girl off her feet?'

Riordan guffawed sarcastically.

'That nasty conniving little rat? As if his face wasn't enough, he had a gamey ankle. If he ever swept any girl off her feet, it wasn't lately, I can tell you that.'

Whilst the two policemen debated, Amy picked at her own meal without appetite. Her head ached, and her whole body was as if drained and exhausted. The joy of settling her differences with Lang had been wiped away by Charlie's unexpected and dramatic arrival, and further dissipated by the fresh evidence that nothing about Hannah was quite as it seemed.

Amy had intended to tell the other what had eventuated during the talk with Mr

Polkinghorne, but now she was angry. Let Hannah find out the truth about the mine for herself! Amy had had quite enough of other women's schemes and of their avid determination to further their own desires. Elspeth's unfeeling impertinence in telling Charles Henthorne that Amy now wished to marry him — and for Charlie to accept this without any word from Amy showed just how featherbrained the poor man was — had left Amy aghast. No wonder he wanted to be off and away as soon as humanly possible. He had made a complete fool of himself at the expense of considerable money and several months of his life.

As she farewelled Charlie the next morning, which was the very least she could do under the circumstances, she had to admit privately that Charlie in defeat was at his best. He showed no rancour, although he did look pale as if he had slept little after the crushing disappointment which had awaited him here in Firebrace.

'I wish you'd stayed a little longer,' she said, quite sincerely. 'If you had met my fiancé, you would have understood better . . .'

'No, no, salt in the jolly old wound. But be happy, Amy. Please be happy,' he implored earnestly, and she felt the tears starting behind her lids.

'If things go wrong, remember that I'm your friend,' he continued in a low but fervent tone.

'Thank you.'

She watched the coach pull out with a strange sensation of finality. This was the break in her ties with her old life. No doubt, she would return on a visit to the Old Country, but it would be as Mrs Firebrace, with a life which no longer touched that of Elspeth.

Amy, lifting her hem discreetly to prevent its being besmirched by the mire of the roadway as she prepared to cross, had no prescience to warn her that she would see Charlie again within three days, and that she would need his friendship, desperately.

Half-way across the street, she was overtaken by Detective Glover, who touched his hat courteously and then plodded off heavily in the direction of the post office.

★ ★ ★

Polly, apparently at a loose end whilst Hannah was out taking her daily walk, came into Amy's bedroom and picked up the dress upon which the girl had been tacking fresh bands of ribbon.

'You're no needlewoman, Miss Amy, that's plain to see,' she chided, in her soft-as-treacle accent.

Amy sensed that the black woman had made this an excuse for conversation, and realised, with some surprise, that this was actually the first time Polly had spoken to her whilst they were alone.

She allowed the other to take the dress from her hands, and, not wishing to appear too curious, attempted a little gentle prying.

'You've travelled a great deal, haven't you?'

'Yes, Miss Amy. We've been here, there, and everywhere. Though's we'd been settled in Brussels when Miss Hannah took a fancy to come out here. Mostly, she doesn't like to go too far from the Duke.' Then she laughed, fine teeth flashing. 'Now, I've let a cat out of the bag, Miss Amy. Don't you go and tell Miss Hannah what I said. Still, secin's we're off soon, it won't matter none.'

Actually, it was plain that Polly wished to brag about Hannah's splendid connections, perhaps to place Amy's moderately rich grazier in the shade.

'He and Miss Hannah are special friends,' she continued, facile fingers plying a needle so expertly that last year's summer dress began to look like a new model. 'He's

223

married, but it's like it is with noble folk. They go their own ways, and his way is Miss Hannah's.'

'I'm really not very interested, Polly,' said Amy, picking up a straw hat. 'Will there be enough ribbon left to trim this?'

' 'Spose so,' answered Polly, rather huffily. 'Not every lady has a friend who could become a king,' she added, just to show how matters stood.

This released Amy from her polite pretence of reserve.

'A king? What on earth are you talking about?'

'Now that Napoleon man's gone, and good riddance, there could be a king in France. And Miss Hannah's Duke could be the one.'

'But why . . . ?' Amy broke off. She knew perfectly well now why Hannah, who could command good money through her stage activities, longed to own a rich gold-mine. There was more than one pretender to the French throne, and perhaps the candidate who could buy the most support would gain the prize. The very idea that the tentacles of European plotting could reach across the world to a tiny town like Firebrace made her want to laugh, and yet, at the same time, something inside was cold and frightened.

She neither trusted nor liked Hannah, but all the while, she had considered that blood was after all thicker than water. Was it?

★ ★ ★

Glover's Saturday was long and hard. It started with long conversations with various persons about the town, went on to a long telegram (charged hopefully against the Victoria Police) sent to a colleague in Melbourne, and filled in the rest of the morning with a ride out to interview Mr Firebrace. Eventually he set out in search of Hannah, or Anna Delacroix as he preferred, whom he found returning from the daily walk which helped preserve her fine figure and resilient constitution.

Hannah needed little prompting to make clear her feelings about Langdon Firebrace. She was angry with her sister for yielding so easily, and now that Amy had defected to the enemy, she was going to push her own case as the only other surviving issue of the late Edmund Felstead. After all, if anything happened to Amy before her marriage, she, Hannah, would be heir to their father's property.

'You're a shrewd woman, Miss Delacroix. What are your idea's about Jane Kestle's

225

murder, the practical jokes, and the rest of it?'

'If this were a play,' retorted Hannah, not missing a step, 'I'd say Mr Firebrace organised the pranks to scare the wits out of my sister so that she'd leave, but then he realised that she was a pretty girl and decided to marry her instead. But Jane threatened to talk, so he killed her. Let's face it, her body might never have been found if it hadn't been for the mine accident.'

'That's a damaging way to talk, Miss Delacroix.'

'I said, if this were a play, Mr Glover. It isn't, you know. A slut like Jane Kestle was bound to end up in bother, one way or another.'

'Where do you keep the pistol, Miss Delacroix?'

Her assurance slipped, but only for a moment.

'Revolver,' she corrected him. 'How did you know?'

'Miss Amy told me about it.'

'H'm. Amy wouldn't know how to use it. It's under my pillow. If you're thinking what I think you are, you can count out the ammunition. It's in a new box, untouched except for what's in the chamber.'

They had reached the end of the main

street, and Glover stopped.

'I won't embarrass you by going further,' he explained. Then: 'I heard you're leaving Monday.'

'Are you going to tell me not to, Mr Glover?' Her head was to one side, her eyes coquettish as she spoke.

'And have you telegraphing to your consul?' said Glover to himself, but he uttered a simple denial. Returning to the police station to write his notes, he pondered on Edmund Felstead's elder daughter. To someone determined to have the Royal Edward for their own, she could be a threat and a nuisance. Yet, Glover had little to back his hunch. What he did have would not impress his superiors. The law needed facts, and all he had was a chance remark, a fleeting impression or two, one missing person, and a few long conversations with certain people here in town.

Unexpectedly, it was Oscar Howarth who gave him a fact to fill out the picture formed during a long, hard Sunday spent mainly in the saddle. He had barely finished his delayed evening meal when Howarth arrived at Riordan's front door, carrying a newspaper.

'I thought I'd better show you this,' he said. 'I've been going through my English papers — y'know, looking for bits and pieces to fill out the *Gazette*.'

The newspaper was ten weeks old, and the item pointed out by Howarth brought a whistle to Riordan's lips.

'So that's what happened to Crafty Sam,' he said. 'Fell off a train. No one knew who he was until his landlady, who was worried about him disappearing when he was paid up for two weeks ahead, saw a piece in a bit of newspaper round her weekend roast about this unidentified man in an Australian suit of clothes and with a badly-set ankle.'

There was another caller soon after, a Chinese hawker travelling westwards. He had a note for Glover, and when the detective read it through, his usual stolidity changed to excitement. Within a few seconds he sobered. He was up against a person of enormous cunning, a remarkable aptitude to convince others that he was something he was not, and a vanity of monstrous proportions.

Glover knew that he had to make a move, and that it had to be the right one.

19

For Amy, sitting in the coach on that steamy morning, preparing to leave Firebrace, everything was unreal. It was all so sudden, and so very frightening. Detective Glover had appeared at her door at seven that morning, as Polly scurried about preparing her mistress and herself for the arduous trip back to Melbourne. He was peremptory and to the point. Polly would go by tomorrow's coach, and Amy would accompany Miss Delacroix in her place.

'But I can't do that!' Amy protested. 'I've a job at Mrs Stacey's school. And my fiancé! Why on earth should I do such a thing?'

She was in the parlour, hastily dressed, facing Detective Glover, who was unyielding and unimpressed.

'Police business,' he said, and then lowered his voice. 'I've reason to think Miss Delacroix might be in danger. If you're with her, she'll be safe, for the time being, at least.'

'Hannah? In danger?' It was all upside down. She had felt in danger from Hannah, that mysterious woman whose life moved along exotic byways.

'I'm serious, Miss Felstead. It'd assist us in our work if you do as I say.'

He was grossly over-reaching his authority, and kept his fingers mentally crossed. Miss Amy was safe, for the time being. Her turn could come later, but now he hoped that his killer would overplay the part. He had to confuse and mislead his prey for a few days longer.

'You write a little note to Mr Firebrace, Miss Felstead, and I'll talk to him, and to Mrs Stacey.'

What would Lang think of her? Yesterday, they had discussed their marriage, which was to be held in the New Year, and Miss Allison Firebrace had softened sufficiently to commence showing her how the household was managed.

Now, after being accepted by Allison, she was bolting with Hannah Felstead, Anna Delacroix if you preferred it, a woman of whom both brother and sister made no secret they disapproved.

The coach had left a hamlet to the west very early that morning, and stopped for three-quarters of an hour at Firebrace to enable its already weary passengers to refresh themselves at the nearby dining-room. The horses were changed, and Amy climbed aboard, while Hannah decided to buy some fruit to eat on the journey. There was not much available at this time of the year, but Hannah said that she felt sure that the store a few doors away had oranges.

Glover, who had been standing a few yards away, hurried across the road in response to a wave from the postmaster. This, he hoped, indicated a reply to his telegram of Saturday, and he expected to be away no more than a minute.

Amy looked out again, hoping that Hannah was returning, for the passengers from points west were emerging from their late breakfast, and the driver was amongst them.

'Charlie! What are you doing here!'

Later, she would recall that all she seemed to do in Charlie's presence was exclaim and wonder.

'Couldn't bear to leave you, dearest girl.' He was gazing up at her with worried adoration. 'But I bring appalling tidings.'

She was out of the coach, being helped down the steps by his well-manicured, yet surprisingly strong, hands. It had never before occurred to her that Charlie, so foppish and ineffectual in his native surroundings of idle social doings, was actually a lithe and powerful man.

'Your friend Langdon Firebrace has been shot. Very serious.'

'Lang?' Was this happening, or was it a nightmare?

'Yes. Dashed lucky I came back. Left the coach half-way to Ballarat. Shouldn't have rushed away like that. Bad form. Had to apologise. Arrived last night and went to your house as soon as decent this morning. The maid told me you were leaving on the coach; couldn't believe my ears. Then I bumped into the doctor fellow next door rushing in to tell you the news. Mr Firebrace didn't turn up last night after he drove you home. Found him at dawn. Frightful affair. I said I'd break it to you gently. Old friend, and all that.'

'Oh, Charlie!' It was all she could say for the moment. Then it began to make sense. 'That was what Mr Glover meant. That man McIntyre has been here all along. He must be a raving madman.'

Charlie Henthorne had her arm and was hurrying her along to a mud-splashed jinker, a horse between the shafts harnessed and ready.

'Doctor said something about a fellow called Beaton. This Beaton person said that Langdon Firebrace killed his girl, your servant.'

'How ridiculous!' She was on the seat, turning towards Charlie as he jerked at

232

the reins. 'It must have been Jack Beaton all along. He has a shocking temper. I know that.'

Meanwhile, Glover had to wait while an enormously long bullock team drawing a heavy wagon passed by, and he rethought the contents of his telegram.

'GLOVER FIREBRACE POLICE STOP HENTHORNE ARRIVED MELBOURNE AUGUST TWENTIETH STOP JOINED EASTERN STAR ADELAIDE FRIDAY WEEK.'

There it was. Proof that Mr Henthorne was a very cunning man indeed, and very eager to lay his hands on the supposed wealth of the Royal Edward. Would the reply to his cable indicate that Mr Henthorne was in financial trouble back in Britain? No matter. That would only be the trimming.

What mattered was that Charles Henthorne had been in Victoria for weeks, and Glover did not doubt that people at an inn at the foot of the Grampians with whom he had spoken the previous day would identify him as the 'naturalist', now minus full beard, who had rashly insisted on exploring those rugged ranges without a guide. Only, instead of gathering botanical specimens, he had been hiding out, perhaps in a deserted hut

233

left by an ebbing gold rush, near the town of Firebrace. He had an ally, a stupid girl called Kestle, whom he had met, probably, in Ballarat as he progressed westwards from Melbourne.

There was still plenty which needed explaining, for instance, the terror campaign directed against Amy Felstead, but, to Glover, Henthorne had seemed a strange person from the first moment of their meeting. There was the peculiar circumstance of a rich English swell travelling without a manservant, and the even odder business of the remark about the Grampians. The name, naturally, suggested Scotland, but how did the vacuous new chum know that those mountains were in fact the Grampians if he had not been in the country before? The actor had been carried away into overplaying his part.

And the matter of the letter which purported to tell Amy Felstead's relative that she had changed her mind about marrying Henthorne. The time factor could not fit. Amy had not been in Australia very long, but the letter had travelled to England and given Henthorne time to come to Victoria. Amy had accepted that her cousin had lied, and had been too upset to question the amount of time for all to have taken place.

So, either Henthorne had been a complete numbskull to believe that a letter had arrived so quickly from Australia, or he was a liar.

'Amy's gone!' said Hannah, standing near the coach with a bag of oranges cradled in one arm.

Glover silently cursed the bullock team.

'She went off with a tall fellow wearing a glass in one eye,' interpolated a nearby lounger, helpfully. 'They got into a jinker over there, and drove off.'

At this moment, Riordan ran up, out of breath, capless, and collar unbuttoned.

'Mr Firebrace has been shot! Where's Miss Felstead?' he panted, and Glover knew, with a cold feeling in his stomach, that he had erred.

He had expected Hannah to be removed first, while Henthorne made another attempt to woo Amy. What he had overlooked was that Henthorne wanted Amy as well as her mine. He was jealous.

The driver of the coach, seated and ready, had run out of patience. First of all Mr Glover had instructed him to keep an eye on the two ladies until they were met by a police officer in Ballarat, and now he was being held up while they all talked their heads off. He called out to the woman and requested that she should make up her mind.

'I'm not going,' cried out Hannah.

'What about the luggage?'

'Oh, confound the luggage!' was the unladylike response.

★ ★ ★

To Amy, watching the horse's ears as it trotted along briskly, the way seemed interminable. Her whole life had stopped with a jolting suddenness, and her lips moved to pray that Lang should be spared and still alive. If he had been shot on the way home the previous evening, he must have lain in the open all night during a drenching thunderstorm.

'Oh, Charlie,' she pleaded, 'do hurry!'

'Doing my best, dearest girl, or rather, the horse is.'

Then:

'Charlie, you've taken the wrong turning. This road goes nowhere,' for he had wheeled the horse sharply from the well-defined track leading to the main gate of the Firebrace property on to a narrow, tree-shaded way.

'No, I haven't,' he said, equably. 'With ordinary luck, Firebrace is dead, and you're mine now.'

She was bemused, but comprehending.

'You, Charlie! It's been you, all along. But

you've only just arrived from England. Why?' Anger rose in her, unreasoning anger which made her, temporarily, very brave. 'You're a murderer. You've killed the man I love. You killed Jane Kestle. And you poisoned poor Mac.'

Irrationally, this last seemed worst of all. She tried to stand and jump from the vehicle, but he grabbed at her skirts and held her firm.

'Don't do that,' he said, sharply. 'I've a gun. I'd shoot you before you ran twenty yards. You're coming with me, Amy, and we're going away to be married. You're a rich girl, and I need your money. Do you understand?'

She understood, and her instinct for survival kept her from telling that she was not rich, and that the mine was worthless. She knew where they were now, approaching the Royal Edward by the same way she had come on that Sunday afternoon when she had met Lang near the entrance.

He made her climb to the ground, and while she stood silent and terrified, he turned the horse and jinker, and, slapping the animal on the haunches, sent it bolting back along the track, the jinker swaying dangerously behind.

'It'll find its way home,' Charlie said

cheerfully. 'I borrowed it, Amy, dear girl, without the owner's permission.'

Sure enough, the horse, recovering from its alarm, settled down to a steady trot, and was soon lost to view behind trees and scrub.

'Let me go!' she cried, and a flock of white cockatoos rose in a whirling, yellow-tinted cloud, their screeching effectively drowning out her screams.

'Be quiet, or I'll kill you. Now hurry.'

She obeyed, shrunken with fear, and when they reached the clear space in front of the mine entrance, he bade her lift away one of the heavy wooden props which kept the boarding in place.

'Now shift those planks in front of you!'

When she had done this, he told her to enter the tunnel. He followed closely, and while she stumbled forward, trying to avoid tripping on the narrow railway which had once carried trucks worked on an endless rope, he found a lamp and matches which he had left on a ledge. When this was alight, he reached out and replaced the planks, thrusting out his arm in the last narrow aperture to pull the prop back into place.

'Walk, Amy,' he ordered. 'It isn't far.'

The tunnel was cold and damp, and pieces of shale rattled underfoot, the sound magnified. There was nothing for it but to keep walking as he instructed, blackness closing behind them as their little glow of light went forward with them. She heard, rather than saw, the water trickling down the walls, and all the while she thought: 'My father died in this terrible place.'

The tunnel opened into a large chamber carved many feet underground. This was the working headquarters of the mine: another tunnel, a mere black circle on the edge of light, continued at the same level. To one side was a shaft going down, a rope-operated platform which had taken miners to a lower tunnel still in place. Water ran down the wall into the shaft, tinkling and gurgling eerily. Wooden beams held the roof of this man-made cave, and as Charlie moved to the centre to hang the lamp from a hook, she saw that the other tunnel extended no more than a few feet. Beyond that was a mass of rubble.

Amy shrank back, and turned away. That was the place where her father had perished as the roof of the tunnel had caved in.

'We'll stay here until night,' said Charlie, amiably. 'I've food stored here. It should be moonlight, and we'll start for Sydney. There are plenty of little mining towns through the ranges where we'll be able to buy horses.'

'You're mad!' she said, the words slipping out before she could stop them.

'Not mad,' he replied. 'I'm a man who can seize an opportunity, dearest Amy.'

'Don't call me that. I'm not your dearest Amy.'

It came to her now that she did not care. Life was running out for her, so why pretend anything but hatred for this monster who, by heaven-only-knew what deception, had embarked on a crazy course of plotting and murder.

'You'll change, Amy. You've always thought me a fool, haven't you?'

She sat on a wooden box, back poker-stiff, throat congested with fear, and grief for Lang tearing at her heart. If Charlie kills me, she thought, at least we'll be together.

'But I'm not. You see, I needed money very badly. My bookmaker was being unreasonable, and I thought I'd ease some blunt out of Uncle Theo. Or Elspeth. She dotes on me, y'know. But on the way down, in my first-class carriage, I found myself alone with the most frightful bounder. A Sam McIntyre. Your father's assistant. He was going to tell you that your father was dead, and help you make a fortune out of the mine. He knew all the ropes, how to raise capital, all of it. I could see what was

240

in his mind. You were a rich heiress and he was after his cut, vulgar little fellow. So I hit him across the back of the neck and took his papers and threw him out of the train. No one knew who he was.'

Her tongue was dry. She could not make a sound.

'When I arrived at the house, there on the salver in the hall was a letter for you from Australia, so I took it. Thought it would be telling you about your father, but it was from him. Your father, I mean. He wanted you to come out. He'd struck it rich at last, he said. I proposed, but you turned me down, you silly girl. But all was not lost. When you heard of your fortune, you decided to rush out here, but by clipper. So I came by steam. Left before you, actually. Travelled second class, grew a beard, and kept my ears open listening to the old colonials coming back to this forsaken country. I'd fed my man some suitable lies before leaving, so that he would cover up for me at that end. Poor old Hawker! Such a faithful fellow!'

Amy found her voice.

'So Elspeth didn't tell you that I'd written to her saying that I'd changed my mind?'

'Of course not. All part of the story, dearest girl. When I arrived in Melbourne, I decided to come west and scout things out. Read

241

something in the newspapers about botanists coming to the Grampians, so I became one too. In Ballarat, I met Jane Kestle. Marvellous luck. Her aunt was looking after your house, and the little fool agreed to ask the old lady to suggest her as a maid for you. It occurred to me, dear Amy, that if you had the wits scared out of you, you'd be so glad to see an old friend that you'd marry me just for the sake of having someone to look after you. Then that stupid girl tried to tell me that I was the father of a child she was expecting. What rubbish! She was that way before I came. Still, she kicked up a fuss and said that if I didn't marry her she'd go to the police and tell them how I'd put her up to scaring you. So I killed her. No other way, dearest girl. The plan couldn't go wrong after all I'd done. Lurking here and there in dirty little huts. Pigging it in here. Quite frightful. But I kept my head. I rode all the way to Adelaide and came back to Melbourne by ship.'

'Was it you who searched my desk? There was nothing of importance there, you know.' She spoke partly to find out more of the truth, and partly to distract his attention as her fingers curled about a loose stone.

'No, Jane did it. Told the stupid chit to make it look as if someone had broken in, to frighten you.' Then, angrily, 'Don't do that!'

His sharp eyes had observed her furtive endeavour, and as his voice rang out and the stone slipped from her grasp, a spurt of dirt fell to the damp floor from the roof.

'Please, Charlie, we must go! It isn't safe in here!' Her idea of knocking him off balance with a stone had gone. All she wanted was the safety of sunshine and clean, warm air.

'We're going to stay until night, Amy,' he said, inexorably, and then, in the soft light from the lamp, she saw him smile, lazily, and yet with sensual anticipation. 'Who knows, you may start to forget Langdon Firebrace.'

20

As he digested the whole disaster of the shooting of Langdon Firebrace and Amy Felstead's disappearance, a fresh voice broke into the thoughts Detective Glover was trying to assemble.

' 'Lo, Mr Glover.'

The speaker was black, white-bearded and grubby, but Glover's recognition was instant, and even at this trying moment, pleasurable.

'Jimmy!' he ejaculated. 'Where did you spring from?'

He knew the other well from the old days. The black had been an official police tracker in those days, and had accompanied the young policeman on many a dangerous trip out into the bush.

'Work for Mr Firebrace now, Boss. Only me 'n' Andy lef'. Res' all dead or on the reserve.'

Glover came to an instant decision.

'Your eyes still good?'

'Too plurry right, Boss.'

Now, to Glover's annoyance, as he prepared to climb into a hastily commandeered dogcart, he found Hannah at his side, ready to accompany them, but he could hardly argue with her statement that Amy could well need a woman's comfort when they found her.

Jimmy was up behind, ready to lend his special gifts to the search. Sergeant Riordan had run across to the post office, to send wires alerting police along the line that a young woman had been kidnapped by a man believed to be a dangerous killer. Constable Price had already departed to commence inquiries into the shooting of Langdon Firebrace, and the only mounted trooper attached to the local force had been away for days seeking some cattle thieves.

They encountered the driverless horse and jinker a mile out of town, and Jimmy, a little further along, pointed out marks showing that the vehicle had turned into a side track and then returned empty. As they progressed along this very narrow road, with Glover concentrating on the reins to avoid overhanging branches, he voiced a question to Hannah.

'When you told Miss Amy you thought a poltergeist was playing those tricks, you were really saying that Jane was the one behind them, weren't you?' She did not reply, so he continued. 'Why didn't you tell her straight out?'

Hannah's expression was faintly outraged.

'I couldn't blacken the poor girl's name without proof,' she said, quite piously. 'I was dropping a hint, that's all.'

Jimmy interrupted to tell them that this was the place where the man and woman had left the jinker, and Glover and Hannah climbed down from their vehicle to follow the black as he pursued what was to his keenly trained vision a clearly marked trail.

'In there,' he said, when within a few yards of the entrance to the Royal Edward.

'Is there another way of getting into the mine?' asked Glover, scratching at his temple under the bowler hat. What to do now?

'Other tunnel all fall in when Mr Felstead die.'

★ ★ ★

Inside the mine, Amy thought that she heard a faint sound in the entrance tunnel. Charlie heard it too, and was instantly alert, gun held steadily.

Hope is a hardy creature, and it fluttered in Amy, inspiring her to bend forward and pick up that same stone which she had found earlier. He swung about angrily.

'Don't,' he snarled, and the gun pointed straight at her.

'Charlie, if you kill me, you wo[...]
to marry me and become owner o[...] was
she said, levelly.

Shale slid down the side of [...]
blocking the tunnel where her f[...] had
died, and despite the chill of this underground
cavern, her body broke out in a sweat under
her thin cotton clothing.

There was another sound, a piece of rock
being kicked by a foot, perhaps, in the
entrance tunnel, and Charlie again aimed
at the dark aperture. Now her desperation
forced her to act calmly, speak sensibly.

'Charlie,' she said, 'look at this piece of
stone. I think there's gold in it.'

He snatched it from her, still pointing his
gun into the entrance tunnel, and held the
rock fragment to the light. Then he laughed,
joyously, crazily, and more shale slithered
ominously.

'It's gold! Do you know, dearest girl, this
is the first time I've seen it in its raw state.
I didn't realise it was right here, under my
feet, and I've been here often enough.'

The glistening band in the piece of stone
fascinated him, and he turned it this way
and that, so that its little lights reflected in
the lamplight.

'I've won,' he said. 'Do you know, Amy,
all my life they've laughed at me. Said I

useless, would go mad like my mother. it I'm going to be rich beyond dreams. I've shown them all, haven't I, and you're going to share it with me, dearest girl. I do love you, Amy. It does matter to me. You shouldn't've said you'd marry that fellow. But he's dead, Amy. I saw him fall and not move again.'

So his mother was mad. *That* had been a well-kept secret, thought Amy bitterly, and she saw Hannah standing a few feet away, their father's revolver firmly in her hand, supported by her other wrist.

Charlie was off guard momentarily.

'Drop that gun,' whispered Hannah, but Charlie was not finished. He grabbed Amy and pulled her in front of him.

What did happen then? Amy was never sure. There was a shot, deafening in the confined space, a reverberation, a cracking, choking dust, pitch blackness, and someone pulling her forward while behind her she heard Charlie screaming as he was caught in the falling rock. Then the screaming stopped as more rock crashed down, and she was being pushed along the tunnel behind Hannah, while Glover, at the entrance, held out his hands to them.

Hannah was as white as a sheet under the dust.

'I thought to distract him,' she stammered. 'I fired at the ceiling. I didn't expect . . . He had a piece of gold in his hand. I saw it. The mine *is* rich, Amy. We were right all along.'

Amy, trying to accustom her eyes to the daylight, hardly heard her. It was barely noon, incredibly.

'It wasn't gold,' she whispered. 'It was fool's gold. He killed for gold, and it was only fool's gold. He killed Lang, and now he's dead, too.'

In a trancelike state, she stared back at the mine, and for a moment did not absorb what Jimmy said.

'Mr Firebrace not dead. Very sick. Not dead, Miss.'

She began running down the slope, unaware of streaming hair, torn and filthy clothing, knowing only that she had to run all the way to the homestead. Several times she had to stop, supporting herself against a tree, whilst she regained her breath, and when she finally reached the gate to the homestead's garden she was too exhausted to push it open.

'Hey!' It was Eric Jago, smelling still of chloroform, who came to her aid. 'What on earth has happened to you?'

'Is Lang all right?' Other explanations could wait.

Dr Jago put an arm about her shoulders and helped her towards the house.

'He lost too much blood, and he knocked himself on the head when he fell, but the bullet's out, and he's resting quite comfortably. He's a strong man, and with you to help him along, he'll soon be well.'

★ ★ ★

In the old days, Glover and Jimmy had worked out a system of signals, based on the ancient aboriginal sign language, and now the detective blessed the silent understanding which had sent the tracker behind Hannah when she had taken things into her own hands. He also had to face up to a new problem, that of Hannah's intentions. Henthorne was dead. Up on the hill, part of the surface had cracked and fallen in, leaving no doubt as to the murderer's fate. But *what* was on *her* mind?

'That was a very near thing for your sister,' said Glover, taking Hannah's arm to help her back to the dogcart.

'Yes,' said Hannah, demurely. The experience had shaken her, but she was too experienced in quick thinking to lose control.

'It's funny what people'll do for gold,' murmured Glover. 'Sad thing about this is that the mine's worthless, anyway.'

She said nothing, so he continued.

'I'll get statements from you and Jimmy as soon as we're back in town. I'll see Miss Amy later. You needn't stay for Henthorne's inquest, Miss Delacroix.'

He did not know whether she had been aware that a possible pistol shot had brought down the rubble which had finished off Edmund Felstead, leaving that wily confidence man, Sam McIntyre, to seek profit in his own way. He did know that this tough adventuress had influenced Oscar Howarth in his attempt to denigrate Langdon Firebrace. Howarth, with the threat of a charge of malicious mischief hanging over him, had been quick to make that clear. But there was no way in which he could prove that Hannah had grasped an opportunity to kill both Amy and Henthorne.

'I feel I should stay. Amy'll need support,' she said, standing aside as Glover unfastened the heavy gate.

'No need for that, Miss Delacroix. You go ahead and take the coach back to Melbourne in the morning.'

For a moment their eyes met, and she

smiled and shrugged in that tantalising way
of hers.

'Perhaps it would be best. I think my gold
is in another country, Mr Glover.'

Briefly, but without mirth, he smiled too.
They understood one another very well.

We do hope that you have enjoyed reading this large print book.

Did you know that all of our titles are available for purchase?

We publish a wide range of high quality large print books including:
Romances, Mysteries, Classics, General Fiction, Non Fiction and Westerns.

Special interest titles available in large print are:
The Little Oxford Dictionary
Music Book
Song Book
Hymn Book
Service Book

Also available from us courtesy of Oxford University Press:
Young Readers' Dictionary
(large print edition)
Young Readers' Thesaurus
(large print edition)

For further information or a free brochure, please contact us at:
Ulverscroft Large Print Books Ltd.,
The Green, Bradgate Road, Anstey,
Leicester, LE7 7FU, England.
Tel: (00 44) 0116 236 4325
Fax: (00 44) 0116 234 0205

Other books in the
Ulverscroft Large Print Series:

HIJACK
OUR STORY OF SURVIVAL

Lizzie Anders and Katie Hayes

Katie and Lizzie, two successful young professionals, abandoned the London rat race and set off to travel the world. They wanted to absorb different cultures, learn different values and reassess their lives. In the end they got more lessons in life than they had bargained for. Plunged into a nightmarish terrorist hold-up on an Ethiopian Airways flight, they were among the few to survive one of history's most tragic hijacks and plane crashes. This is their story — a story of friendship and danger, struggle and death.

THE VILLA VIOLETTA

June Barraclough

In the 1950s, Xavier Leopardi returned to Italy to reclaim his dead grandfather's beautiful villa on Lake Como. Xavier's English girlfriend, Flora, goes to stay there with him and his family, but finds the atmosphere oppressive. Xavier is obsessed with the memory of his childhood, which he associates with the scent of violets. There is a mystery concerning his parents and Flora is determined to solve it, in her bid to 'save' Xavier from himself. Only after much sorrow will Edwige, the old housekeeper, finally reveal what happened there.

BREATH OF BRIMSTONE

Anthea Fraser

Innocent enough — an inscription in a child's autograph book; a token from her new music teacher, Lucas Todd, that had charmed the six-year-old Lucy. But in Celia, Lucy's mother, it had struck a chill of unease. They had been thirteen at table that day — a foolish superstition that had preyed strangely on Celia's mind. And that night she had been disturbed by vivid and sinister dreams of Lucas Todd . . . After that, Celia lived in a nightmare of nameless dread — watching something change her happy, gentle child into a monster of evil . . .

THE WORLD AT NIGHT

Alan Furst

Jean Casson, a well-dressed, well-bred Parisian film producer, spends his days in the finest cafes and bistros, his evenings at elegant dinner parties and nights in the apartments of numerous women friends — until his agreeable lifestyle is changed for ever by the German invasion. As he struggles to put his world back together and to come to terms with the uncomfortable realities of life under German occupation, he becomes caught up — reluctantly — in the early activities of what was to become the French Resistance, and is faced with the first of many impossible choices.

BLOOD PROOF

Bill Knox

Colin Thane of the elite Scottish Crime Squad is sent north from Glasgow to the Scottish Highlands after a vicious arson attack at Broch Distillery has left three men dead and eight million pounds worth of prime stock destroyed. Finn Rankin, who runs the distillery with the aid of his three daughters, is at first unhelpful, then events take a dramatic turn for the worse. To uncover the truth, Thane must head back to Glasgow and its underworld, with one more race back to the mountains needed before the terror can finally be ended.